## Praise for *Being Esther*

"Karmel's novel of womanhood, the love and strife between mothers and daughters, marital dead zones, and the baffling metamorphosis of age is covertly complex, quietly incisive, and stunning in its emotional richness."

—Donna Seaman, *Booklist*

"Deeply moving . . . Karmel's subtle, psychologically acute rendering of Esther's life reveals a woman who has lived fully, if not flamboyantly; loved deeply; kept her dignity, irrepressible wit, and essential humanity. *Being Esther* is a spare book with cosmic implications and a huge heart."

—*Lilith Magazine*

"The author writes the story of Esther past and present with remarkable tenderness. Readers of any age will long for more Esther."

—*ForeWord*

"*Being Esther* is a poignant story that will be told more often as the population ages . . . rightfully depicted by Miriam Karmel as a tale worth telling and reading."

—Miriam Bradman Abrahams, *Jewish Book Council*

"Karmel's accomplished debut illustrates the bittersweet truth that we live our quotidian lives and we worry about the manner of our leave-taking, but if we're lucky, we come to understand, as Esther does, that despite our bewilderment at finding ourselves old, 'our lives are enriched by the minor interactions that present themselves every day.'"

—*Minneapolis Star Tribune*

"*Being Esther* is a poignant, true-to-life portrait of a woman growing old that will linger long in readers' minds and hearts."

—MaryAnn Grossman, *St. Paul Pioneer Press*

"That Karmel, who is younger than 85, could capture so well the inner life of the old is a tribute to her powers of observation and empathy. That she could express this life with such clarity and wit is a tribute to her writing skill, for *Being Esther* is anything but a dirge. It is a delight."

—Neal Gendler, *The American Jewish World*

"A novel about an eighty-five-year-old widow living in suburban Chicago may not sound irresistible, but thanks to Karmel's beautifully precise prose, her absolute fidelity to her characters and their vicissitudes, and her keen wit, *Being Esther* is impossible to put down. What a wonderful debut."

—Margot Livesey, author of *The Flight of Gemma Hardy*

"*Being Esther* is a small masterpiece, every detail unerring. I wanted Esther to move in next door so we could play two-hand bridge and mix drinks with names like South Side Sling or Not Your Aunt Nellie. I would coax her to tell me about the boys before Marty and about the Starrlights. In Esther, Miriam Karmel has created a character one will never forget nor ever stop loving."

—Faith Sullivan, author of *The Cape Ann* and *Gardenias*

"Miriam Karmel's Esther is such a lively and attentive companion that I loved viewing the world through her eyes. Her acuteness challenges anyone who imagines aging only as diminution and a fading sense of self. Looking back, looking forward, Esther is curious, wryly funny and always (sometimes painfully) honest."

—Rosellen Brown, author of *Before and After*

**Being Esther**

# Being Esther

*A Novel*

Miriam Karmel

milkweed
editions

Published 2013 by Milkweed Editions
Printed in the United States of America
Cover design by Christian Fuenfhausen
Cover image © Margie Hurwich/Arcangel Images
Author photo by Richard Migot
13 14 15 16 17   5 4 3 2 1
*First Edition*

Milkweed Editions, an independent nonprofit publisher, gratefully acknowledges sustaining support from the Bush Foundation; the Patrick and Aimee Butler Foundation; the Dougherty Family Foundation; the Jerome Foundation; the Lindquist & Vennum Foundation; the McKnight Foundation; the voters of Minnesota through a Minnesota State Arts Board Operating Support grant, thanks to a legislative appropriation from the arts and cultural heritage fund; the National Endowment for the Arts; the Target Foundation; and other generous contributions from foundations, corporations, and individuals. For a full listing of Milkweed Editions supporters, please visit www.milkweed.org.

Library of Congress Cataloging-in-Publication Data

Karmel, Miriam.
    Being Esther : a novel / Miriam Karmel. — 1st ed.
       p.    cm.
    ISBN 978-1-57131-105-4 (acid-free paper)
    1. Older women—Fiction.  2. Self-realization in women—Fiction.  I. Title.
    PS3611.A7839B45 2013
    813'.6—dc23

                                                                          2012025933

**Milkweed Editions is committed to ecological stewardship.** We strive to align our book production practices with this principle, and to reduce the impact of our operations in the environment. We are a member of the Green Press Initiative, a nonprofit coalition of publishers, manufacturers, and authors working to protect the world's endangered forests and conserve natural resources. *Being Esther* was printed on acid-free 100% postconsumer-waste paper by Edwards Brothers Malloy.

*To Bill*
*and for Shirley*

*my friend said face it that's how it goes one by one*
*till there's no one left on this bench in the sun*

—Grace Paley

**Being Esther**

## Prologue

They named her Esther.

As a child, Esther believed she was named for the Persian queen who risked her life saving her people from a wicked man. Every year, on the holiday commemorating that miraculous rescue, children in costume flock to synagogues to hear the story of Esther. They rattle noisemakers whenever the wicked one's name is uttered; they hiss and boo. Esther had loved parading around her shul in a long dress, lipstick, and a tinfoil crown, pretending to be the fearless, noble queen.

When she was older, Esther enjoyed telling people that she'd been named for Esther Williams, which, given her age, was impossible.

The fact that Esther was named for neither the famous swimming beauty nor the savior of her people was of no concern to Esther's mother, who simply shrugged and said, "I don't remember" whenever Esther asked the origin of her name. If Esther were to plead with her mother to remember, Mrs. Glass would merely say, "Oy, please. Can't you see I'm busy?" Then she would instruct Esther, in Yiddish, to go play in the street or go hit her head against a wall.

One day, worn down by Esther's nagging, Mrs. Glass finally allowed that Esther had been named after Esther Jo Berman, the daughter of Mrs. Glass's best friend, Lottie. Not that she was named *for* Esther Jo. But when Esther was born, a better name had not presented itself. "It seemed like a good idea at the time," her mother said.

The truth came as a disappointment. Still, Esther was grateful that her parents hadn't given her the middle name of Jo. She could almost hear her father say, "What kind of name is Jo for a Jewish girl?"

And so she was Esther, with no middle name.

Recently, Esther has begun to wonder whether her life might have turned out differently had her name been deliberately chosen. Not that anything untoward had befallen her. She'd raised two healthy children; traveled some. Sometimes she wishes she had done more, had a career, like her daughter and granddaughter. Yet she's wanted for nothing. It even embarrasses her to think that people might envy the ease with which she has sailed through life.

Still, she can't shake the feeling that if only her parents had named her with intention, she might have grown into her name, as if it were an inheritance that mustn't be squandered. Instead, Esther has gone through life with a borrowed name, like some off-the-rack garment or counterfeit designer handbag, a name like the fake Seiko watch she purchased on a trip to Mexico with her daughter, Ceely, whose name had been deliberately chosen.

Five people. The Markels, should they answer, will make six and seven.

Esther has been working her way through the alphabet, phoning the numbers in the tooled-leather address book her mother once brought back from a temple tour to Israel, one she'd picked up in the souk and gave to Esther for her twenty-ninth birthday. It took Esther a year before she dared to write on the creamy vellum, making the first entries with the silver fountain pen her mother-in-law had given her as an engagement present. Soon enough, she was using anything at hand—pencils, ballpoints, felt-tip pens that bled through to the other side.

Now the pages are riddled with slashes. In fifty-five years people move—like the Markels, who left Chicago for Phoenix after Buddy retired. Her sister Anna moved so often Esther had to start a second page, though she still hasn't drawn a line through Anna's last entry, the place on Fourteenth Street in Santa Monica.

Esther makes her calls from the kitchen table, where she can gaze out the window at the changing sky or at the pedestrians passing by. In the other direction she can see, across the divider into the living room, the few familiar furnishings she and Marty had moved from the house on Shady Hill Road—the mahogany breakfront, one of the matching love seats they'd bought on sale at Marshall Field's, the red leather easy chair, a couple of paintings.

The gilt-framed mirror that used to grace their old foyer is now wedged onto a patch of wall between the two small rooms.

They'd moved the old rotary phone, too. Esther prefers it to the infantilizing portable phone with the oversized buttons that Ceely gave her for Mother's Day. She misplaces it. And she finds it disconcerting that she can be anywhere—even the bathroom—while speaking to some unsuspecting person on the other end. Besides, she enjoys the mild exertion of rotating a dial, the steadying effect it has on her trembling hand.

The Markels' phone is ringing. Esther resists the urge to hang up, telling herself the odds are in her favor; this time somebody will answer. Twice already, as she has worked her way through the book, answering machines have informed Esther that the number she dialed was, in fact, the number she dialed. The first time she got a machine she panicked and hung up. The second time, she was prepared. "Hi! This is Esther Lustig. Remember me? I was just calling . . ."

Then Marty interrupts. Even in death his gravelly voice intrudes. Essie, Essie. After all these years, a person doesn't call just like that. Out of the blue. Use your head.

Setting the receiver down, she looks across the table, as if her husband were sitting there working the crossword puzzle or finishing his second cup of coffee. "And why not out of the blue?" she demands.

Marty is forever looking over her shoulder, monitoring her every move, offering unsolicited advice. After he died, after she left him at Waldheim on that bitter afternoon wrapped in his flimsy prayer shawl, left him with the gravediggers who were off to the side, not so patiently revving their backhoes as the last mourners tossed dirt on his coffin, after all that, she had expected that finally she'd get some peace and quiet. Not that she doesn't miss him. Marty's absence is palpable.

Now she consoles herself that friends lose touch, not intentionally, but because eleven years ago you made a mental note to give someone a call and then the days slipped by. Of course, that wouldn't satisfy Marty, who always had to analyze every little thing, examine it from this angle and that. If Esther lost her temper, burned a pot roast, forgot to pick up the dry cleaning—he would draw a line clear back to her childhood.

While the Markels' phone rings, Esther glances at her leather book, the blur of lines running through the names. What if Sonia isn't there?

Gently, she sets the receiver back in its cradle. The last number she dialed had been reassigned, though Esther still wasn't ready to draw a line through Charlene Fink's name. And when she phoned Sadie Sherman, Emily answered, all grown-up and pleasant enough, though Esther still recalled the colicky baby who had grown into a churlish child and then an insubordinate teen. Emily informed Esther that she and her sisters were sorting through their mother's belongings. "Mom moved to assisted living last month." Windy Shores or Cedar Hollow—the name sounds like the overnight camps the children once attended. Esther tries picturing Sadie, who'd run a successful travel agency for twenty-nine years, making lanyards or pot holders or clay pinch pots.

Esther takes a deep breath as she prepares to redial the Markels. She hopes that Sonia will be the one to pick up, though at this point it will be a relief to get anyone on the other end, even prickly old Buddy. BM, they'd called him behind his back.

The phone rings twice. Three times. Four. She is about to hang up, when someone answers. A man. "Hello!" she blurts. "This is Esther Lustig calling." When the man doesn't reply, she repeats her name, and then, always quick on his feet (Buddy and Sonia were remarkable dancers—tango, cha-cha, rumba, you name it), Buddy cries, "Esther! Esther Lustig! Is that really you?"

Giddy with excitement, she practically bursts from her seat, as if they were rushing headlong to embrace. "I suppose it is!" she exclaims, her hand flying to her head as if to affirm her identity. Oddly, she feels reassured by the soft nimbus of hair, which is as familiar as the sound of her own voice. Then she catches her reflection in the old gilt-framed mirror. There she is, the same basic model: green eyes, coppery-blond hair, broad forehead, and the full mouth, which she has been painting the same shade of red since college. With her free hand, she adjusts her silver glasses and recalls Marty saying that when she removed them she looked like Judy Holliday. After Marty got sick she let the blond go, but the steely gray reminded her of cloistered nuns, and soon she was coloring it again.

She's held on to her figure, more or less, carefully selecting her garments to compensate for the less. Other than the loss of an inch or two—she stands just a bit over five feet—everything is the same. Yet nothing is. She has become a caricature of herself.

"Yes, it's me," she sighs, sinking back into her chair. "It's Esther. Esther Lustig."

Then Marty is back, accusing her, in a high-pitched falsetto, of behaving like a schoolgirl. I suppose it is. Esther. Esther Lustig.

Placing her hand over the receiver, she tells him to shut up. "Am-scray! Get out of my hair!"

"What was that, Esther?" Buddy says.

"The cat," she lies. "He was clawing the sofa."

Animated by her anger and pleased with the convincing riposte (Buddy wouldn't know, but Sonia would, that Esther loathes cats, that she once drove the family tabby, who'd been clawing the furniture, to a secluded ravine off Sheridan Road, where she released it into the wild), Esther launches into her spiel, the one she's been honing since the first few awkward calls. She no longer lets on that she is going through her address book, checking to see who is here and who has gone to the other side. After that rather indelicate attempt at gallows humor fell flat, she started telling people that she's been sorting through boxes of old photos. "And you'll never guess what I came across," she says.

The picture she describes to Buddy was taken at a college dance. "Sonia's in it," she tells him. "Along with me and Ruthie and Helen. We were the Starrlites. With a double *r*, like Brenda Starr! And that silly play on *light*." They'd adored Brenda, she tells Buddy. "She was so thoroughly modern, and she had that boyfriend with the mysterious eye patch and the dashing name. Basil. Basil St. John." Esther repeats Basil's name, as if she were under a spell induced to unleash ancient memories. She studies the picture. There they are, the four Starrlites—and their dates. Was it on a dare that they'd all hopped up on the bandstand during the musicians' break and mugged for the camera, pretending to play the instruments? She's forgotten the names of the young men, except for her date—Jackson Pflug. Who can forget a name like that? Sonia will remember the others, though she probably won't recall any better than Esther how they'd managed to round up four men in those days. Esther probably encouraged Jackson to dance with the girls who came alone because she remembers dancing with Sonia, wishing she were with Marty, who had been shipped off to Holland shortly after they'd met. Sonia smelled faintly of lily of the valley, and when Esther rested her head on Sonia's shoulder and felt Sonia's sweet, warm breath on her neck while the band played "I'll Be Seeing You," she was glad Jackson was dancing with some other girl. Poor Jack. In two months, he would be killed in the Siege of Bastogne.

"I don't know what got into us," she tells Buddy. "You should see Helen, perched on the piano, legs crossed, open-toed shoes peeking out from under a long, flowing skirt. Remember Ruthie? She's blowing a sax. I'm at the drums. And Sonia. Sonia is hugging the bass, beaming. Her hair is swept up to one side, with a flower pinned in it."

"A flower!" Buddy exclaims, as if he's never heard anything so extraordinary. "What kind?"

"Why, I don't know," Esther stammers, irritated that he'd ask about a flower, rather than the name of Sonia's date or even what Sonia was wearing, until she remembers that Buddy is a landscape architect and might reasonably wonder about such things. Then it occurs to her that Buddy is retired, in which case it might be more accurate to say, "He was a landscape architect." Is. Was. She wishes there were better road maps for growing old.

Lately, Esther has been preoccupied with such thoughts, though she keeps them to herself. If Ceely knew, she'd have her in assisted living faster than you can say "Bingo!" Esther plans to die first.

Buddy is still going on about the flower. Should she make something up? Gardenia? Orchid? Esther's earliest (and unhappy) exposure to flowers occurred during the two weeks each summer when her parents rented a room in the Dunes from Mrs. Zaretsky, a sharp-tongued woman who used to come tearing out of her kitchen, apron flapping, to scold the children in Russian if they got anywhere near her dusty flower bed. Later, when Esther and Marty started to travel, she expanded her understanding of flora, but it was mostly limited to the names of plants that grew abundantly in sultry places—bird-of-paradise, calla lily, jacaranda.

Hastening to change the subject, she reports that Sonia is wearing an embroidered blouse with flounce sleeves. "It's the kind you might bring back from a foreign market," she tells Buddy. "Then one day, you see it hanging in your closet and wonder, 'What on earth was I thinking?' But Sonia had flair. On her, it doesn't look like a costume."

"Sonia's uncle lived in Mexico City," Buddy says. "Her folks drove down there once a year. They'd return with a carload of silver pins and bracelets, straw chairs for the children, wool shawls, and embroidered blouses. Lou had dreams of starting an import-export business."

"I remember," Esther lies. Then she reminds Buddy of the winters their group spent in San Miguel. Every January, once all the kids were in college, the Starrlites and their husbands took rooms at the old Aristos Hotel. They set up house for a month, with their toasters and coffee pots and electric fry pans. In the evenings, they gathered for cocktails.

"Sonia made the best margaritas," Esther says.

"It was the limes," Buddy remarks, and suddenly Esther remembers how stingy he'd been with praise. It wasn't the limes, she wants to say. Instead, she asks if he remembers the parrot that lived in the Aristos courtyard, and when he says, "Can't say that I do," she decides she's had about all she can take of Buddy Markel.

It was time to put Sonia on. She'll remember. What's more, if Esther were to say, "Parrot," Sonia will mock the bird and cry, "Hola!" And Esther will feel as if she's come home, that at long last she's returned to the place where you don't need reminding that the front door sticks or the toilet handle needs jiggling or the third runner on the staircase is loose. Sonia will recall how the parrot squawked until Lolita, the hotel's duenna, fed it breakfast.

Then Esther will say, "Papaya and banana."

"Yes," Sonia will exclaim. "The same fruits she left in baskets outside our doors each morning."

"With the bread."

"From the *panaderia* down the road!"

Sonia will remember it all. She'll vouch for Esther's memories; she will validate Esther's existence.

The first time Sonia followed Esther home after school, a carp, which Esther's mother had bought at the kosher market on Kedzie Avenue, was swimming in the bathtub. Esther hadn't wanted Sonia to see the fish flopping around in the rusty tub. She'd already been to her friend's home where Sonia's mother had been seated at a desk writing letters on pale blue stationery, a cardigan with pearl buttons draped across her shoulders. Esther told her new friend that until the fateful day when her mother knocked the fish out with a wooden mallet, chopped it up, ground it and shaped it into fish patties, she loved perching on the toilet seat and reaching into the tub to feed it bits of lettuce and crusts of bread. "It was the closest thing we ever had to a family pet," she confessed.

The carp had fascinated and delighted Sonia, who'd never known anyone who made gefilte fish from scratch. And though Esther knew such people existed (her family mocked and pitied them), she hadn't known anyone who bought the fish in jars.

Sonia will remember it all: Esther's aversion to cats, the parrot, the fish, the names of those grinning young men.

"Put her on," she says to Buddy. "Put Sonia on."

"Oh, Esther," he moans.

A heavy silence engulfs the space between them. How could she have been so reckless? So presumptuous? Put Sonia on! As if they were in Mexico and she just dialed the Markels' room (they always stayed in number 7).

Yet she can still hear the squawking parrot, taste the papaya, smell the sweet *panaderia* breads. She has been so transported by memory that when Buddy says, "I'm afraid that won't be possible," Esther expects him to explain that Sonia has run out to the market for more limes.

Ceely wants Esther to move to Cedar Shores. After Marty died, Ceely started placing glossy brochures on Esther's coffee table, her nightstand, and even tucked between the pages of her latest book. The other day, she held one open and pointed to the pictures. "Look, Ma. You'll have your own room. There's even a small kitchen. But you won't need to bother. There's a dining room for all your meals." The dining room tables were draped with white cloths. Mauve napkins bloomed from water goblets.

Esther's old friend, Helen Pearlman, who'd loved martinis, cooked with lemongrass, and played a mean game of tennis, is stashed away in a studio apartment at Cedar Shores, where they serve blush wine before dinner on Saturdays and hold nightly bingo games in the party room. Once a week a bus arrives for anyone wanting a ride to the supermarket.

Not long ago, Esther visited Helen. The two women sat across from each other on matching mauve love seats in the "family room," straining to talk above the din of the TV. Actually, Esther held up both ends of the conversation, while Helen's attention drifted between Oprah and a group of card players at a table near the bay window. Esther asked Helen if she'd heard about Oprah's great car giveaway? "Everyone in the audience got a brand-new Pontiac," she said. When Helen's eyes brightened, Esther thought she'd guided her friend safely back home through the fog. Then Helen said, "You know, Esther, I finally divorced Jimmy," and Esther wondered whether there was any point in reminding her friend that Jimmy had been dead for eleven years. When Helen said, "He came home with powder on his shirt one too many times," Esther rose, kissed her friend's papery cheek and said goodbye.

No. Esther is staying put. She has no intention of joining her friend in Bingoville. "Thank you, very much," she told Ceely, as she handed back the brochure. "I'm happy just where I am."

She and Marty moved here not long after Ceely ran off to a commune in Vermont. Barry was in dental school. The move back to the city had been Marty's idea. Gamely, Esther agreed, though not before spending a day in the basement crying into a pile of freshly laundered towels.

She'd loved her old house, but the city proved to be a tonic. Esther and Marty felt freer, lighter, as if city living was like one of the miracle diets Esther was always trying. They enjoyed learning their way around the new neighborhood, though it was very near to the one they had left years ago when they joined the great migration north to the suburbs. They discovered the joy of walking—to restaurants, the hardware store, movies, the library.

They rediscovered the joy of sex. Marty referred to that time as "our second honeymoon," but to Esther, their couplings felt nothing like their early awkward intimacies. She and Marty became eager and playful, but also patient and considerate with one another. At the same time, their sex felt X-rated, illicit. Esther enjoyed pretending they were lovers sneaking off for an assignation in a borrowed room. In bed, she felt as if she were somebody else, somebody she would like to know. Suddenly she was that somebody! Nothing had prepared her for how good she would feel.

Then one day, Marty said, "I can't believe we wasted all those years living in the sticks."

Esther, who couldn't believe she'd ever cried into the towels, hated to think that she'd frittered away her life. "Wasted?" she frowned. "Let's just say it was nice while it lasted." She reminded Marty of the trees that formed a canopy over the quiet roads; the expanses of green; the tranquil village where the children could ride their bikes to the playground or the ice cream parlor and she never had to worry. And hadn't they made interesting friends? She was forever entertaining, and like-minded people reciprocated. "It felt right at the time," she told Marty.

"I hated every minute of it," he declared, at which point Esther retreated to the kitchen and started chopping onions for a pot roast.

Esther refused to let Marty ruin her joy. She had few regrets about the past, and she took pleasure in the present. She'd loved everything about their new life, even the building's name. The Devonshire Arms was a typical Chicago-style building—three wings, four stories, dusty yellow brick. Yet she appreciated the fact that there were no lingering cooking smells in the hallway as there were in her sister-in-law Clara's building, where garlic, fried meat, and scorched oil seeped into the hallway carpets, the wooden lintels, the paint on the wall. Not once has Esther smelled the curries from the Singhs' apartment across the hall.

And what a surprise and a pleasure it was to encounter Lorraine after all these years, in an apartment across the courtyard. Next door to Lorraine lives a young boy who practices piano every morning and sometimes at night. In the summer, with the windows open, Esther feels as if she is being serenaded.

And if she asks Milo, the super, to fix a leaky faucet or change a bulb in the hallway, he responds as if he's been waiting all day for her call. No. Esther isn't moving. What's more, she'll have no part in her daughter's get-out-and-do-more campaign. Ceely wants Esther to join the mall walkers, take up water aerobics or yoga. Just the other day, while unloading a bag of groceries in Esther's kitchen, Ceely remarked that a friend's eighty-four-year-old mother had taken up tai chi and still mowed her own lawn.

Ceely has always tried to improve Esther. When she was ten years old she hounded Esther to play mah-jongg with the other mothers. And why didn't Esther wear eyeshadow and get her hair done once a week like Susie Gordon's mom? And did she have to wear a sweatshirt and corduroy slippers around the house? Ceely had a way of making Esther feel like the old love seat they'd moved to the basement rec room after the stuffing started to show.

All these years later, Esther is still on the defensive. "You wouldn't believe how much exercise I get just walking around the house," she said, as Ceely finished unpacking the groceries. "Besides, I don't have a lawn to mow." She reminded her daughter that she walked to the library and the drugstore and that she and Lorraine walked to Wing Yee's on a regular basis. She walked to the market on Devon a few times a week. Though she doesn't need much, Esther enjoys steering a cart up and down the aisles, examining all the products that weren't available when she was a young woman running a busy household. The year she took up Chinese cooking, she drove halfway across Chicago for gingerroot and five-spice powder. Now, when she has little appetite and nobody to cook for, she can load her basket with five kinds of goat cheese, purple peppers, yellow tomatoes.

"The supermarket doesn't count," Ceely said, as she stuffed the empty bag under the kitchen sink. She called grocery shopping an "add on," something Esther would do no matter what. "You need to do more," she declared.

And if I don't? How can Esther tell her daughter that some-times she is content sitting by the window, looking out at her neighbors coming and going, or staring across the courtyard and watching Lorraine's cat sunning itself on the windowsill? She can sit without her knitting or a book. She is content doing nothing, and she can't explain why.

Esther is an avid reader, though she rarely purchases a book. She prefers checking books out of the library, where she can exchange pleasantries with the librarians and hear them say, "These will be due in two weeks."

Sometimes, though, as she leaves the library, Esther's delight turns to fear as she imagines her father trailing after her, wagging an accusing finger and issuing a stern admonishment: "Don't you forget, Esther. No lunch is for free."

How long has her father been gone? Yet still, his voice wins out. She has even imagined arguing with him, trying to explain that the books are in fact free, if only for a few weeks. "It's a lending library, Pa."

Still, whenever she approaches the exit, she expects one of the librarians to come running after her, shouting, "Hey! Where do you think you're going with those?" But she keeps walking, never looking back, until she is safely at home. After bolting the door, she collapses onto the sofa and waits for her breathing to return to normal, for her better self to prevail, and for the earlier frisson of fear to be replaced by an overwhelming sense of pleasure. Her father was wrong.

Esther was a young married woman when she bought her first book. *Nine Stories* was on the best-seller list, and she couldn't wait to be in on the excitement. When Betty Pink, the librarian, informed Esther that fifteen people were ahead of her on the waiting list, she headed to Kroch's and Brentano's to purchase a copy. The fact that the surly clerk had never heard of J. D. Salinger and ignored Esther's attempts at conversation didn't diminish her pleasure at the thought of owning her own copy. Then, while handing her money to the clerk, Esther started at the sound of her father's voice. "Aha!" he said, as if he were standing there beside her. "I told you, 'No lunch is for free.' Now maybe you'll believe me."

Esther felt unsettled after reading the stories, not unlike the way she'd felt after smoking her first cigarette or drinking her first cocktail. It was as if she'd reached some defining moment, some point of no return, after which she'd never be the same. Yet when she looked in the mirror, the same open, candid face stared back at her. And when she spoke, a familiar, soft voice filled the air. The metamorphosis, if that's what had occurred, left neither visible nor audible traces. Yet somehow, she felt transformed.

Those nine stories were like a road map to another world, one populated with precocious children and confused adults. There was even a character with the surname of Glass, though he bore no resemblance to any of the Glasses in Esther's family.

Connecticut, practically a character in one story, seemed as alien and distant to Esther as the Polish shtetl from which her parents had fled. After reading the story about two women from Connecticut who spent an afternoon drinking, Esther couldn't stop thinking of her mother scrubbing the kitchen floor, polishing the Shabbes candlesticks, chopping onions for soup. She had no frame of reference for this newly delineated map of the world.

Esther hated the way Eloise from Connecticut treated her maid, as if she were nothing more than a stick of furniture. And it broke Esther's heart, the way Eloise ignored that darling child of hers, with the imaginary playmate, Jimmy Jimmereeno.

Jimmy Jimmereeno!

The story haunted Esther. While peeling potatoes for dinner, she saw those two women sipping highballs in Eloise's well-appointed Connecticut living room. As she washed the lettuce, she heard the sound of clinking ice cubes and slurred female voices. By the time she set the table, she was feeling like one of the old dresses in her closet, something outmoded that she'd hung onto for too long. After putting the children to bed, Esther soaked in the tub longer than usual. She wondered if she knew anyone to invite for drinks in the afternoon.

The next day Helen Pearlman stopped by.

Esther, who had just popped a roast in the oven, hugged her friend and said, "How about a drink?"

"Coffee would be great," Helen replied. "But only if you've got some made."

Esther, annoyed with her friend, wondered how Eloise broached the matter of drinks, since a first round had been poured offstage, so to speak, sometime after Mary Jane's arrival and before the clinking of ice cubes in empty glasses. Of course, Esther would know just what to say once she and Helen had finished their first round. "Gimme your glass." That's what Eloise had said to Mary Jane.

Esther told Helen that she had something different in mind. "A highball, perhaps?"

"A highball?" Helen consulted her watch. "At two thirty?" She laughed so hard she cried. "Oh, Esther. You're such a card. That's what I love about you." Wiping tears from her eyes, she said, "If you have any cream, I'll take just a splash."

Later, as Esther cleared away the coffee cups, she told herself that nothing good could come of drinking in the afternoon. After all, look at how Eloise had treated that precious child, and how she'd disregarded the feelings of the maid, and how she and Mary Jane had slurred their words. Still, her hand trembled as she wiped cake crumbs from the table. While rinsing the dishes, Esther wondered if she was missing out on something. Yet she was busy raising Barry and Ceely; she helped Marty with the pharmacy books. What more could she want?

Not long after Helen refused to drink a highball in the afternoon, Ronnie Kaufman, the accountant who lived two doors down, ran out for a pack of cigarettes and never returned. Ronnie's defection was the most exciting thing that ever happened in their neighborhood, inspiring all sorts of speculation ranging from another woman to sudden amnesia to kidnapping. But Ronnie was no kid. Looking back, it was easy to see that when a thirty-nine-year-old man with a wife and three children fails to return home from the minimart after running out for a pack of Lucky's, he was a victim of nothing but his own lack of imagination, his inability to envision a better way of breaking free from the monotonous, suffocating, mind-numbing tedium of his world, which was bounded by the greenest, most neatly manicured, chemically enhanced lawn in the entire post-war suburban development known as Timber Ridge.

As if Ronnie's disappearing act wasn't enough, Marty came home one evening, poured a scotch without ice, then polished it off before telling Esther that his assistant's wife had been fooling around with her tennis instructor. Everyone was getting in on the act, even that shiksa, Effie Greenberg.

Esther, who had been planning to tell Marty that she'd just accepted a part-time job at Kroch's and Brentano's, decided to wait until after dinner before breaking the news.

She'd been peeling potatoes that afternoon and quizzing Barry on his spelling words when the phone rang. She was

annoyed with Barry, who'd failed his last test. And the potatoes had sprouted. She wiped her hands on her apron before
picking up the phone. "Yes?" she said, with the abrupt impatience of a person ill-suited to dealing with the public.

Yet she got the job. "Monday. Of course," she stuttered.
"Thank you."

Esther had convinced herself that the interview hadn't gone well.
She'd worn—in the end—the suit she wore last year to her nephew's
bar mitzvah, with brown pumps and a matching leather handbag.
At the last minute, thankfully, she'd stuffed the gloves in her purse.

Penny (even her name was playful and blithe) had on a soft
pink sweater and a slim gray skirt. Her shoes, skimming her feet
like ballet slippers, were the color of doves.

They'd sat on either side of Penny's desk, in an alcove near
the back of the store. The space was barely large enough for a
desk, a small bookshelf, and the chair under which Esther hid
her matronly handbag from view. Esther, who'd worked summers at her father's dress shop, had never interviewed for a job.
She folded her hands in her lap and attempted a smile.

Helen had coached Esther, said she'd be asked about her
goals. "My goals?" Esther eyed her friend with suspicion. "You
know," Helen shrugged. "Where do you see yourself in five
years?" Esther let out a nervous laugh. Her goal that day was to
pick up Marty's suits at the cleaners; make sure they hadn't run
out of milk; drive Ceely to her piano lesson. "What am I thinking?" Esther said to her friend.

Penny didn't ask about goals. She skimmed the application
Esther had spent hours preparing, pushed it aside, and said, "I
need someone three mornings a week."

Was that a conversational gambit, an opening through which
Esther was expected to reveal something of herself? She eyed

Penny's casual, blond hair, the way it stayed within the confines of a thin plastic headband. Eloise would have hair like that. You remind me of Eloise, she might say. And then they could discuss the story about Connecticut. The other stories, too, if there was time. Penny would see that Esther loved to read, was up on the latest books. So what if she couldn't imagine a life beyond the one she was living?

"And I need someone who's punctual." Penny tilted her head to the side, as if she were assessing Esther's ability to read a clock. "Is there any reason you can't show up on time?"

Esther shook her head. Ceely and Barry would be in school by then, Marty long gone to the pharmacy, leaving her to rattle around, holding down an empty fort. She wanted to tell Penny that she'd fly to the store; walk the two miles, if the car broke down. Nervously, she nattered about working in her father's store. She neglected any mention of dusting the mannequins, polishing the mirrors, filling the cut-glass dish with lemon drops, and chose instead to inflate her duties in the office, where, in a pinch, she opened the mail, sorted the accounts payable, answered the phone.

On the basis of that, she supposed, she got the job.

Marty was stretched out in his favorite chair working the daily crossword when she finally spoke up, announced her good news.

"But what about the children?" he said, without glancing up.

"What about them?" Esther absentmindedly flipped through a magazine, wishing she could find a way to tell her husband how she'd been rushing to get home before school let out when she spotted the help-wanted sign in the window. She might share with him that she changed her clothes three times before the interview, and still got it wrong. "But I got the job!" she could say.

"Basil's girlfriend," Marty said, pressing a pencil to his lips. "Six letters."

She glared at him as she recalled an earlier conversation, one in which she'd proposed returning to school for a degree in library science. "Then what?" he'd said. "Then I'll get a job at a library," she replied. "At your age?" he asked. Esther was thirty-three. This time, Esther intended to stick to her guns. Marty wasn't going to bully her out of a job.

She set the magazine down and picked up *Nine Stories,* which she'd been displaying on the coffee table for weeks. "It's only three mornings a week," she said. "While the children are in school," she added, her voice trailing off.

Flipping to the last story in the book—the one in which that brilliant child was pushed into the deep end of an empty swimming pool—she settled on the passage she'd committed to memory. Esther had read and reread those lines as if she were rehearsing for a play. She recited them in front of the mirror and while clearing the breakfast dishes. "One of these days you're going to have a tragic, tragic heart attack." That's what the woman in the story, the one with the unfortunate son, had said to her husband. Esther shouted those words while she ran the vacuum, while making the beds. Then, like that fictional woman, she threatened to wear red to her husband's funeral and sit in the front row flirting with the organist.

Esther was conjuring a way to work those lines into the conversation, the way to portend Marty's death and his funeral, when he looked up from his puzzle and said, "I suppose if it's only three mornings a week . . ."

Esther closed the book, returned it to the coffee table, and nodded. "Brenda," she said.

"Brenda?"

"Basil's girl." Softly, she added, "Nobody will ever know I was gone."

Every morning at 8:30 sharp, Esther and Lorraine speak by phone, though it would be easy enough to meet near the statue of Saint Francis, in the building's courtyard.

One morning Lorraine makes the call, the delicate expression the two employ for checking to see that the other has made it through the night. The next morning, Esther returns the favor. And so it will go, until the day one of them doesn't answer, leaving the other to panic, wondering what to do. Dial 911? Call Milo, the building's super?

Today, while waiting for Lorraine to call, Esther peers through her living room window across the courtyard into the other apartments of the Devonshire Arms.

Lorraine's curtains are drawn, yet Esther can picture her friend seated at the kitchen table with the *Sun-Times* and her second cup of Sanka.

When the phone finally rings, Esther picks up and without so much as a hello, says, "Ceely kidnapped me."

"Esther, listen to me. Your own daughter cannot kidnap you."

"Trust me. She did." Esther pauses, waiting for her friend to deliver the verbal equivalent of a pat on the arm.

Lorraine sighs. "To tell you the truth, I didn't sleep so well."

"I just said that I was kidnapped, and you're going on about a sleepless night!"

Esther is about to hang up when Lorraine says, "Why don't you start at the beginning?"

"Not now," Esther whispers. "Later. I'll tell you at lunch." She has just finished reading the newspaper. The government is spying on ordinary citizens, listening in on phone conversations without a warrant. Though she doesn't believe for a minute that anyone would bother eavesdropping on a couple of eighty-five-year-old women, she isn't taking any chances. What happened to her is nobody's business.

She thinks about her grandson, Josh, who doesn't care who knows what. Last Sunday, after dinner, he sat her down at his desk, punched some keys on his computer, and told her about something called a blog. "Here, Nonna. Check it out." She read about Josh and his girlfriend, a sweet girl with a heart-shaped face and messy hair, about the things they did when he was away at college, about the smell of his sheets after sex. Esther, who could remember changing Josh's diapers, stopped reading and said, "Very nice."

No, she is not about to broadcast the details of her life to strangers. No blogs. No revelations for government spies. "I'll tell you everything. Later," Esther says to Lorraine. "Now tell me what kept you up. Was it the music? I heard him playing again last night."

Sometimes at night Esther listens for the music from across the courtyard. The autistic boy who lives next to Lorraine can play for hours. It's always the same, a haunting melody that stirs forgotten feelings of longing. This she won't tell a soul, not even Lorraine, but last night the music started when she was in bed reading. She set down her book, closed her eyes, and listened. When the music stopped, she opened her eyes and he was there, standing at the foot of her bed. "So it's you," she said, smiling up at him. Marty's hair appeared as thick and wiry as the first time they'd met. He needed to lose the same ten pounds he'd carried before his illness. And he wore the same fat, sloppy grin. Even the gap between his front teeth, the one she'd loved exploring with her tongue, was still there.

"Yes," he said, jingling the change in his pockets. "It's me."

"The music," she said. "It touched me."

"Where?" He drew closer. "Show me."

She placed her hand on her breast, and he placed his hand over hers, and then he began moving it slowly up and down the front of her body, playing her with the assurance of a virtuoso. She closed her eyes again and tried guessing what song he was playing.

When she opened her eyes he was gone and she wept at the loss, which felt as strong as the first time. Then, her hand touching the spot where his hand had been, she whispered, "If that's what you get to do after, if you get to learn to play such music, then maybe it's not such a bad place after all. Better than that joint Ceely's been pushing."

Now Lorraine is saying, "It wasn't the music. I just couldn't stop thinking about poor Mrs. Singh." She pauses. "Or maybe it was the cake I ate at dinner. Maybe that's all it was."

"No," Esther says. "What happened to that woman is enough to keep anybody up."

Esther has never had a neighbor like Mrs. Singh, who lands, unbidden, at Esther's door, a bird-of-paradise in her brilliant saris bearing samosas, lentils with curry, chapatis, and dal.

Esther knows that cooking is her refuge from the loneliness of being shut in with a sick husband. Yet lonely as she is, Mrs. Singh has never accepted Esther's invitations for tea. "Kumar," she'll say, looking over her shoulder at the door she always leaves slightly ajar. "Well, next time," Esther will say. Graciously, she accepts her neighbor's offerings, always returning the empty plates with something of her own creation: poppyseed cookies;

chicken soup; a wedge of her famous kugel, the fat, buttery egg noodles studded with plump golden raisins.

Now she confesses to Lorraine that until the other day, her biggest fear for her neighbor was that she would trip on the hem of her sari and fall down the stairs. "There must be some way to hike it up," she tells Lorraine. "Even in winter, she lets those beautiful silk skirts drag through the snow."

"The Singhs owned a shop on Kedzie," Lorraine offers. "Before Mr. Singh got sick. It was one of those shops that sell saris and gold."

"That's no excuse," insists Esther, who knows that about the Singhs. "Dresses aren't like tissues, no matter how many you have."

Over lunch at Wing Yee's, Esther tells Lorraine that the other day she'd gone down for the mail and found Ceely in the lobby with Milo. "They stopped talking when I showed up, and gave each other a look. I was sure he'd been telling her about Mrs. Singh. That's the last thing I want Ceely to know. I felt like chasing her out the door with Milo's broom. Then Milo started whistling and sweeping the stairs, and Ceely asked if I was ready. I didn't know what she was talking about." Esther pauses. "Remember *Gaslight?*" She searches Lorraine's face for some sign of comprehension. Amazingly, Lorraine's looks haven't deviated since high school. She wears the same coral lipstick and her hair, swept up and secured into place with a thick coating of spray, is still a silvery blond. Esther always feels as if she has a poppyseed stuck in her teeth when she's with Lorraine.

"You don't remember, do you?" Esther says. "It's the movie where Charles Boyer convinces his wife that things that happen are figments of her imagination. He isolates her and in the end he drives her mad." She pauses. "Lorraine, I am here to tell you that my daughter is gaslighting me. She insisted that we had a date. But we did not."

Lorraine nudges a teacup toward Esther.

Esther pushes it away. "You don't believe me."

"I believe you." Lorraine refills her own cup. "But she didn't exactly kidnap you. She's your daughter. Besides," she says, reaching across the table for Esther's hand.

"Stop!" Esther recoils. "I know what you're going to say—that I don't have to move. But one day . . . one day, just like Helen, I'll paint my eyebrows with lipstick, or serve a raw roast to dinner guests. I'll burn myself with the teakettle, or trip on the bath mat and break my wrist. We have to be so careful, Lorraine. It's exhausting being this careful."

Mrs. Singh was mugged early on a Sunday morning, while heading for a bus to visit Mr. Singh in the hospital. She'd hoped to arrive in time to feed him his breakfast.

"Next thing I knew, I was on the ground," she tells Esther, who already knows the details, compliments of Milo. The two women have run into each other in the foyer, collecting their mail. Mrs. Singh's arm, the one she ordinarily uses to hike up her sari when she climbs the stairs, is in a sling. As she struggles with the key to her mailbox she tells Esther that she never heard her assailant. "One minute, I'm heading for the bus; the next, boom, I'm on the ground!" All she remembers is a burning sensation piercing the shoulder where her purse strap had been. Her sari was ripped, her eyeglasses broken, and so was her right arm, which had taken the brunt of the fall. "I never saw it coming," she says.

Esther considers telling her neighbor about the mugging that precipitated her father's move to America, and how he often reminded the family that if he hadn't been attacked at the train station in Warsaw by a group of hooligans who taunted him for being a Jew, he would have gone to the death camps with the rest of his family. Her father spoke of that attack as "the straw that broke the camel." Sometimes, he called it "the silver lining in the clouds."

Instead, Esther offers to help Mrs. Singh in any way she can and warns her neighbor not to trip on the hem of her sari as she makes her way up the stairs.

Safely back in her own apartment, Esther bolts the door and fastens the chain, and thinks that if Ceely ever gets wind of the mugging she'll put her in that place where Helen Pearlman is stashed away. Esther can't find the silver lining in what happened to Mrs. Singh.

Shortly after Mrs. Singh was mugged, a sign went up near the mailboxes in the foyer announcing a meeting in the courtyard near the statue of Saint Francis, on Wednesday at five. A police officer will be on hand to answer questions and address concerns about neighborhood safety. The sign says: "Bring your own chair."

Esther plans to bring one of the lawn chairs that she and Marty had found on sale at Walgreens alongside a jumble of rubber flip-flops and tanning oils. When Marty suggested that they buy two, she'd pictured the patch of dirt between the sidewalk and the curb that Milo rakes and waters to no avail. "What will we do with lawn chairs?" she asked. Marty paused, jingled the change in his pockets, and said, "You never know." Then Esther pointed to a spot where the plastic webbing was starting to fray and said, "They won't last a season." Now five summers have come and gone. The chairs have lasted longer than Marty, who'd hung them from a hook on the wall in the basement storage room.

When Esther goes downstairs to retrieve her chair she wonders whether Mr. Volz, who lives in the apartment one flight up from hers, can use the other one. She isn't sure why she thinks of Mr. Volz, except that he doesn't own a car, and while that doesn't preclude him from owning a lawn chair, she regards him as a man with deliberately few possessions. It also occurs to her that this is an opportunity to get to know her neighbor better. She already knows, from the sounds he makes padding around in the rooms above hers, that he is an early riser with regular habits. She knows, from Milo, that he does something at the university involving rare books, though she can't imagine what. Perhaps he has girlfriends? Or not. There is something in the way he tosses his scarf as he slides into a taxi each morning that suggests she might want to tread lightly where that is concerned.

Milo carries the chairs upstairs, setting one in Esther's foyer and leaving the other propped outside Mr. Volz's door. Then Esther phones her neighbor to explain. The answering machine picks up and she realizes she's never heard his voice, for whenever they pass in the hall Mr. Volz simply nods.

"This is Esther Lustig. From downstairs," she tells the machine. She considers describing herself so that Mr. Volz won't confuse her with Mrs. Singh or with that boorish Ella Tucker in 3A. But what could she say? I'm short and appear to be getting shorter. I have blond hair, though I've noticed that in a certain light, it looks pink. I wear eyeglasses with silver frames. My husband used to say that I look like Judy Holliday. If we were at a party, he'd wrap an arm around my shoulder, smile, and say to anyone within earshot, "She's a dead ringer for that broad, don't you think?" People would nod and look down at their feet. Once, to relieve the tension, I joked, "He's only saying that because I beat him so badly at gin." But that merely added to the discomfort, so I described the scene in *Born Yesterday*, where Judy Holliday beat Broderick Crawford in gin. People coughed and studied their feet again. Later, I told Marty that if he ever pulled that stunt again, I'd leave him.

Finally, Esther finds her voice. "I live downstairs in 2B. I left the chair for you. In case you're going to the meeting tomorrow evening." The machine cuts her off before she can say that she'll understand if he doesn't use it. She dials again, but as soon as she hangs up, she realizes that she's forgotten to leave her phone number. Then she writes a note.

Dear Mr. Volz,
Perhaps you can use this chair for the meeting tomorrow. It's been in storage for too long. I'm glad to share it.
Sincerely,
Esther Lustig, 2B

She rereads the note, puts it in an envelope, seals it, and on the outside, in her best Palmer script, writes: Mr. Volz. Then she trudges up the stairs, holding tight to the railing. After pausing for breath at the landing, she tapes the note over a part of the webbing, which, as she'd predicted, has come undone.

The next morning, Esther discovers the chair propped outside her door. Taped to it is an envelope with MRS. LUSTIG printed in neat block letters.

When Esther makes the call to Lorraine that morning, she describes how her hand shook as she opened the envelope. "I felt like one of those stars at the Academy Awards. The paper is thick," she says. "Real quality."

"Esther! Please, just read the note," Lorraine insists.

"Hold your horses." Esther presses the paper to her bosom. "I'm getting there. You know," she says. "You weren't always so impatient."

"And how would you know?"

Esther is silenced by this truth. She and Lorraine had gone their separate ways after high school. All those years Esther was busy raising a family in the suburbs, Lorraine was here, sharing an apartment with her mother. For thirty-five years, Lorraine rode the el to an office on LaSalle, where she worked as a legal secretary.

Mrs. Garafalo kept house. Lorraine has told Esther that every Saturday morning she had her hair done at a salon on Montrose, after which she and her mother went to Marshall Field's for lunch. On Sundays, they went to church. And in the evenings? But Esther has learned not to press Lorraine about life with her mother. She has never found a way to ask, Didn't you want to strike out on your own? Instead, the two women picked up where they left off, on graduation day at Von Steuben High, all those Junes ago. Recently, Lorraine said, "When I'm with you, Esther, I forget that we're no longer in high school. It's as if all those years in between never happened." The confession, so unexpected, so out of character, stopped Esther from turning the moment into a joke, from suggesting that a mirror would help bring back all those years.

"Okay," Esther sighs. "So you were impatient. I didn't know. Now, do you want to hear the note?"

"Go ahead," Lorraine says.

Esther clears her throat, holds the letter out at arms length, and reads:

Dear Mrs. Lustig,
Thank you for the kind offer of your chair. Alas, I have a prior engagement and am unable to attend the meeting.
Yours truly,
Timothy Volz

"Timothy," Esther says. "You don't hear that very often."

"Well, you don't see him very often, either. Odd man," Lorraine replies.

"I don't know what you're talking about."

"I'm not going to spell it out for you, Esther. And do you really think he has a prior engagement? Prior engagement! Who says things like that? 'Busy.' He might have said, 'I'm busy.'"

"People get busy," Esther snaps.

She hangs up and thinks about Timothy Volz and his prior engagement. When was the last time she had to decline an invitation because she was busy? She is beginning to feel like an old Eskimo drifting away on an ice floe, passively observing all the busy people back on shore. There are so many ways that people keep occupied. Perhaps Mr. Volz is traveling. Then she wonders if she is too old to travel and if not, where would she go?

Shortly after Helen Pearlman's move to Cedar Shores, Esther decides to pay a visit. She has in mind taking Helen out to lunch, perhaps to that sushi place her friend enjoyed so much. But by the time Esther pulls into the Cedar Shores lot a heavy rain is threatening to put a crimp in her plans. One mishap on a rain-soaked road and Ceely will take away the keys quicker than Esther can say Bingoville.

Helen's door is ajar as if she were expecting a visitor, though Esther hasn't called ahead. "She won't remember that you're coming," warned Helen's daughter, Fanny.

Helen stands gazing out the window, where a pair of cardinals, oblivious to the rain, dance around a feeder. Her white hair sticks out in wispy tufts, sprouting haphazardly to expose patches of baby-pink scalp. Her faded muumuu has slipped off one shoulder, revealing a bone structure as delicate as a prepubescent girl's. She isn't wearing a bra.

Esther, dressed in a navy-blue pants suit with a polka-dotted silk blouse, feels like an officious staff social worker or a volunteer delivering magazines and good cheer rather than a childhood friend who can show up wearing any old thing.

"Yoo hoo!" Esther taps on the open door. "Anybody home?"

Helen turns and regards her friend.

Fanny told Esther that recently her mother painted her eyebrows with lipstick. Today, however, Helen's pale face is a blank slate, static and impassive. Yet beneath the wreckage, Esther detects the outlines of a beautiful woman.

"Helen?" Esther utters her friend's name, as if she's just run into someone she might have known, but isn't sure.

Helen turns back to face the window. Her spine is beautifully straight and as Esther lets herself into the room and crosses to the window she reminds herself that her friend's mind, not her body, is giving out.

Esther places a hand on her friend's narrow back and kisses her papery cheek. Once Helen had returned from France smelling of lavender; she'd discovered a new perfume.

"How are you feeling today?" Esther asks.

Helen presses her nose to the glass and mutters something Esther can't understand.

Esther remembers her plans for lunch. What had she been thinking? Tentatively, she touches her friend's arm. "So you're feeling all right?"

"Rude bird," Helen says, as a jay dive-bombs the cardinals. "Dumb, too, out in the rain like that. Never did like them."

When Fanny reported the lipstick incident, she also mentioned that the Cedar Shores staff was threatening to move her mother to a more secure part of the building. Apparently Helen had been speaking in a French accent, and though Fanny didn't understand why that was a problem, she was told that it was a sign of some sort of disorder affecting her brain—Fanny couldn't remember the name—and that her mother's behavior was becoming increasingly erratic. Recently, Helen had accused Consuela, a uniquely competent aide, of stealing one of her boxes of cherry Jell-O. Helen buys the Jell-O on outings to the supermarket and lines the boxes up on a bookshelf, as if she were assembling a set of encyclopedias, one volume at a time.

The next day, when Consuela knocked to remind her about breakfast, Helen said, "I don't want to go to ze dining room."

Now Helen turns to Esther and, sounding like the girl who'd shared a locker with Esther for four years at Von Steuben High, says, "I had a sneaking suspicion you'd show up. It's good to see you, Esther." She smiles and strokes Esther's cheek, peering into her eyes with a knowing look. She points to an easy chair, gesturing for Esther to sit, then perches on the edge of the bed.

"Wait!" Esther cries. "I'll get you a chair." Quickly, she sees that other than a straight-backed wooden chair tucked under a small dining table, she and Helen have exhausted all the options. Dejected, Esther settles back down. Helen's cramped room looks nothing like the pictures Ceely has been pushing. The narrative set out in the glossy brochure invites Esther to imagine sipping coffee on her patio while watching golfers tee off on the third fairway. Esther is meant to believe that she will spend her days hitting golf balls on the Cedar Shores links, or riding the shuttle to the mall. In the evening, she'll sip wine before dinner with a sleekly handsome, silver-haired man. There is a strong presumption of sex. Nothing in the brochure hints at the pungent aroma of beef broth and Lysol that assailed her when the sliding glass doors parted open to the lobby. The smell followed her all the way down the hall to Helen's room, where it has worked its way into the curtains, the bedding, the walls. Helen's home had smelled of lavender and fresh-cut flowers. Her living room was cluttered with books and magazines and there was always plenty of seating, even if some folks had to sit on the large, brocade pillows Helen stored under the piano. She was a generous hostess and didn't mind experimenting with new dishes on her guests. Nobody ever left her home hungry.

Now she apologizes for not having anything to offer Esther.

"Not even tea or coffee." She smiles ruefully. "Or a drink. Wouldn't that be fun!" She claps her hands in delight. "Remember Sonia's margaritas?" Her eyes light up, as if their old friend has just handed them a long-stemmed blue glass with a salted rim. "But I'm out of tequila." Helen holds up her empty hands and frowns with regret. Then her face lights up; her blue eyes sparkle. "Maybe we'll run out and get some. The good stuff."

Esther nods and wonders if lunch is a possibility after all, though perhaps a Mexican restaurant would be more fitting.

"Remember the time Marty ate the worm from the tequila bottle?" Helen throws her head back and laughs. "How many drinks had he had by then?"

"I didn't speak to him for three days," Esther confesses.

Helen's eyebrows shoot up. "Because he ate the worm?"

That was so many years ago. Esther can't remember why she punished her husband with silence. Certainly not because he ate the worm. Or had she? If only she could do it over. She'd be less quarrelsome, more agreeable. She shakes her head. "I honestly don't recall."

"Well, you must have had your reasons," Helen says, as if discerning Esther's need for forgiveness.

Suddenly, shouting erupts from down the hall. A look of alarm crosses Esther's face as she glances at the open door and then back to Helen, who appears as unruffled as she'd been gazing out at the birds. A man, presumably not the silver fox depicted in the brochure, is ranting, and several aides go rushing past Helen's room, apparently to quell the disturbance.

"Oh, that's just Mr. Kelner," Helen says, dismissing him with a wave of her hand. "He's a shouter. Every day, around this time, he shouts for his keys. His wife died last year, but he still thinks he has to pick her up. She was standing in front of the beauty parlor waiting for him, when something, I can't remember what you call it, fell off the building and hit her. It was one of those freak accidents."

Esther nods. "Cornice," she says, as if she were helping Marty with one of his crosswords. "I remember reading about that in the paper."

"Cornice?" Helen leans forward and squints at Esther, who hopes she hasn't triggered a lapse into French or some other fog. But Helen continues with her story. "By the time Mr. Kelner arrived, there were ambulances and rescue squads all over the place." She pauses. "I guess his mind stopped that afternoon."

When the commotion next door finally subsides, Helen asks about Ceely and Sophie. "And that hotshot dentist son of yours." She leans forward, as if they are already at lunch, sharing secrets across the table. "Tell me everything," she says, and Esther thinks the sushi place might work after all.

Esther glosses over Barry's financial troubles and mentions that her granddaughter has a new boyfriend. "Sophie's found another loser, I'm afraid. She's bringing him to dinner soon. I'll know more after that." She is beginning to feel like a foreign correspondent, reporting from a distant shore. Or is this how it feels to visit someone in prison? How much do you tell a person whose life is so constrained, without stirring feelings of resentment or despair? She hesitates before deciding to tell Helen that she's been thinking of taking a trip somewhere. "Maybe to Mexico." Esther doesn't say that Ceely has been trying to get her to move to Cedar Shores and that she suspects the trip could be her last hurrah.

"Mexico!" Helen claps her hands again and smiles. "You can pick up a bottle of tequila. But without the worm."

"One bottle, without worm," Esther says, relaxing into her chair. Their exchange is so effortless, so light and easy, like old times. Then before she knows it, she hears herself saying, "I understand you've been speaking with a French accent."

"French?"

"Oui!" Esther replies, still in a playful mood.

Helen blanches; her mouth tightens. "Where'd you hear that?"

"Fanny," Esther mumbles, fearing she's said too much.

"She's my daughter."

"I know." Esther flashes a nervous grin.

"What do you know?" Abruptly, Helen rises and makes her way back to the window.

Esther remembers when Helen took a crash course at Berlitz. Then, after returning from Paris, she bought a stovetop espresso pot at a shop in Old Town and sweet-smelling cigarettes from the stand in Evanston that sold out-of-town newspapers and the racing gazette. After her French phase, Helen did nothing but knit mohair shawls. For a while, she was consumed by baking yeast breads, and then she planted a perennial garden.

In all those years, Helen had never turned on Esther, who is staring down at her hands as if they might hold the answer to what just transpired. Her hands flutter in her lap like the birds outside the window. She seizes one with the other, hoping to steady them. Then, looking up at her friend, she says, "I see there's a party here on Saturday night." Her voice sounds shrill, too bright. "There was a sign in the lobby."

Helen taps on the glass until the birds fly off. "I used to throw a party," she says. "Shrimp de jonghe. I served shrimp de jonghe. They cried for more. Remember?"

Esther remembers the year everyone served the fussy shrimp dish. Francois Pope demonstrated the recipe on TV and the next day there was a run on seashell ramekins at cookware shops across the city. She made it once and loved how the house smelled of garlic and herbs, until the image of her mother's pursed lips and her father's wagging finger intruded and broke the spell. Her father's voice followed her around the kitchen, then into the dining room as she presented the dish to admiring guests. *Trayf! Trayf!* he cried, chanting the word for the forbidden food. Once, Esther confessed to Helen that she couldn't get his voice out of her head. "He sounded like a barking dog. *Trayf! Trayf!*" Helen threw back her head and laughed. "That's such hocus-pocus, Esther. Nobody keeps kosher anymore."

Esther had envied the ease with which Helen could turn her back on tradition, the same ease with which she wore long, blowsy dresses, garments with a decidedly ethnic flair—muumuus the year Hawaii was granted statehood; dashikis when black power was in the ascendancy; gauzy skirts in the manner of hippie flower children. When the group began wintering in Mexico, Helen started a fad with brightly embroidered shifts, though she alone managed to look like something other than an overstuffed chintz sofa.

Now, in a faded muumuu, her nose pressed to the glass, Helen is nattering about a dish that Esther has long forgotten. "Shrimp de jonghe," she says, as she taps on the window. "Shrimp de jonghe. Shrimp de jonghe."

Esther is wondering whether Helen is slipping into her French fixation, when Mr. Kelner starts up again. "Keys! Keys! Where the hell are my goddamn keys?"

Suddenly, Helen turns from the window, her face wild with fear. "The keys," she cries, crossing the room to the closet. "They're in my purse." And before Esther knows what is happening, Helen is at the door, her muumuu sliding off one shoulder, a worn leather handbag dangling from her wrist.

"Where are you going?" There is panic in Esther's voice. She remembers her plans for lunch, how she'd imagined Helen slipping into her coat, the two of them making their way down the corridor, then sailing through the parting glass doors to Esther's car. Helen would slide into the passenger seat, Esther would pull out of the parking space, and off they'd go to Edo Sushi, where Helen would order a bento box and Esther would pick at anything on the menu that wasn't raw.

"Are you coming, or not?" Helen stomps her foot. She is wearing pink slippers, the kind that might have been crocheted by one of the denizens of Cedar Shores.

"Oh, Helen." Esther doesn't know what else to say. Then Mr. Kelner resumes his shouting, and again an aide comes racing past Helen's door.

Helen, her face flushed with impatience, ignores the commotion and continues stomping her pink foot. "Let's go!"

Esther considers calling the aide who is rushing toward Mr. Kelner's room, then above the din she hears a jay's scratchy cry. "All right," she says, and without considering where she'll get the seed, she suggests going outside to fill the feeder.

"Greedy jays." Helen sounds frantic. "I feed people. We'll get shrimp. At the Jewel. Write that down, Esther. Shrimp. What else? What else do we need? Did you write that down?"

With trembling hands, Esther fishes a slip of paper from her purse and writes *shrimp* in shaky block letters. She is holding the note out to Helen when the aide, who'd earlier rushed toward Mr. Kelner's room, pops his head in the door. "Everything okay?" He's a short muscular young man with a shaved head. "You all right, Helen?"

"No!" Helen cries, stomping her foot again.

The aide enters. With his gaze fixed on Helen, he tilts his head toward Esther. "Is she bothering you, Helen?"

Helen stares blankly into space and when she shrugs her muumuu slips farther down her shoulder. Esther has an urge to set it back, cover her friend's exposed flesh. But the young man has insinuated himself between the two women, creating a gulf that Esther could never breach.

He turns to Esther. "We can't have you disturbing the residents." He shouts, as if he's determined that Esther is hard of hearing.

"Excuse me?" Esther, whose hearing is just fine, is both startled and annoyed by this officious young man's cheek. Next, he'll be advising her to remain silent, tell her she has the right to an attorney.

"We can't have you disturbing the residents." He crosses his arms over his chest, narrows his eyes at her.

"But we're old friends," she insists. "We've known each other since we were young girls. Children." Her voice brightens as she seizes on what might be a winning argument. "We were children together!" She wishes she possessed a document attesting to her history with Helen. There must be something—like a passport or driver's license—something to legitimize her right to be here, some proof she could press on this overbearing man with the glinting gold ring in his left ear.

"I'm sorry, ma'am." He lowers his voice, but she can tell that he is not sorry at all. And then he says, "You have to leave."

"Leave?" She avoids his gaze, looks over his shoulder toward the window. "But we were just on our way out. To feed the birds."

"I'm sorry, but we can't have you disturbing the residents," he says, as he ushers her toward the door.

She pulls away from him, loses her balance, but steadies herself against the doorframe. She fingers the buttons on her blouse and smoothes her skirt, before turning to face him. She has put up with enough from this man with the muscles and the shaved head. "You're not sorry at all," she says. "And Helen, my friend Helen, is not a residents." She hisses the final *s*. "Helen is a resident. Singular. One person. Unique. But how would you know? You look at her and all you see is an old woman in a faded, loose dress. But that dress, which is far older than you, happens to be a muumuu. Helen brought it back from Hawaii. Before Hawaii was even a state."

Esther stops. Her heart feels like it will pop the polka dots off her blouse. She clutches her purse to her chest and turns to Helen, expecting to see mirth glinting in her eyes, dancing around the corners of her beautiful mouth. Helen will defend her from this interloper. "Brava!" she will say. "Brava, Esther." But Helen has assumed her gone-to-the-moon look; she is lost from the inside out.

Esther blows a farewell kiss to her friend and, holding her head high, brushes past the aide and out the door.

Perhaps she only imagines it, but as she makes her way down the hot, fusty corridor, she hears Helen call out, "Au revoir, Esther!"

Esther was delighted when Marty's mother gave her a cookbook as a wedding shower gift. It was not just any cookbook, but the best-seller by the famous Popes, Antoinette and Francois, who by then had influenced a generation of Chicago housewives.

Esther, who was not a suspicious woman by nature, regarded her mother-in-law's gift as an obvious choice for a young bride. But in time, Toots Lustig (her real name was Mildred), a fancy cook herself, revealed her true intentions. She expected her new daughter-in-law to provide her son with the kind of meals to which he was accustomed.

Toots was known for her fancy butter cookies, as well as for her chopped-liver swan, a sleight-of-hand extravaganza involving tinfoil, sprigs of parsley, and sliced pimento olives, strategically placed to resemble eyes. Toots once invented a casserole—a mélange of pasta, canned tomatoes, green pepper, and gobs of Velveeta cheese—which she dubbed "Jewish spaghetti," though it was neither inherently Semitic nor Italian.

One afternoon, Toots invited her new daughter-in-law to watch while she baked butter cookies for a bridge party she was throwing with her two sisters. (Esther, under her breath, referred to the women as "The Gabors." Not that they were glamorous, but Toots and her sisters shared a kind of haughty fake grandeur affected by that Hungarian trio.)

While Toots prepared the cookies, Esther watched from across the table, as she'd done so often in her own mother's kitchen.

Unlike Toots, Esther's mother never consulted a recipe. In fact, not until Esther received the cookbook from Toots had she considered how instinctively her mother prepared the dishes that had been passed down from one generation to the next, as if she hailed from a primitive culture with an oral tradition. Mrs. Glass threw in a bit of this, a bit of that, tasting as she went along.

Toots lined the cookie sheets with small chunks of dough and chatted in such easy tones that only later did Esther feel the sting of her mother-in-law's acid tongue. "Marty isn't like you, Esther," Toots said, as she gently rocked the back of a fork over a spoonful of dough, creating decorative ridges like shoes leaving impressions in freshly fallen snow. "My son doesn't have the stomach for peasant food," she said, in the same even voice she might have used to report that she'd just run out of milk.

Then with her free hand, she picked up a burning cigarette (there was always a burning cigarette) and took a drag without, miraculously, Esther thought, dropping ashes onto the dough. Squinting at Esther through a cloud of smoke, Toots said, "You understand what I'm saying, don't you?"

Esther nodded. And though she was too young and inexperienced to understand what Toots was up to, she sensed it was best not to reveal that the first time she brought Marty home for dinner, he ate two helpings of her mother's luxen kugel. And when he agreed to an extra serving of brisket, her mother turned to Esther and beaming, said, "He eats like a horse!"

Mrs. Glass prepared homely food, in shades of brown and beige—thick soups with barley and lima beans, heavy poppy-seed cookies, noodle puddings that sat in your stomach for hours. Beet borscht, the lightest dish in her repertoire, happened also to be the most colorful. Even her desserts—yeast cakes with plums, stewed figs, and prunes—were as drab as the shtetl from which she hailed. Still, Esther believed that blind-folded, her mother's cooking would have earned blue ribbons at the state fair.

Yet Esther never learned to cook at her mother's side. The few times she asked how to prepare a dish, her mother would shrug and say, "You shid a rein," which sounded like something one would not want to associate with either the preparation or the consumption of food, but which merely meant throw in a little of this, a bit of that. Each of her mother's dishes was an improvisation, a jazzy riff, a variation on a theme. Like snow-flakes, no two were alike, yet each iteration was remarkably similar to the one that preceded it, and each was received with pleasure.

And so Esther, who could neither shid a rein nor bake a but-ter cookie, started marriage with a handicap her mother-in-law clearly intended to rectify.

Esther prefers not to think of her early experiments with cooking when, shaken by Toots's remark about Marty's delicate stomach, she enrolled in the Antoinette Pope School of Fancy Cooking.

By the time Esther arrived (she took two buses and walked six blocks), Madame had measured the ingredients into Pyrex bowls and lined them up, in order of their introduction into the dish du jour, on a long counter that looked more like a bench in a chemistry lab than the red Formica table in Esther's kitchen.

Esther came prepared to roll up her sleeves and put on an apron. But Madame did all the cooking. Once again, Esther found herself sitting on the sidelines.

At the first class, Antoinette, or Madame, as she preferred to be called, demonstrated how to make marble cake by running a chocolate swirl through the center of a pound cake. In time, Madame demonstrated egg rolls, shrimp de jonghe, and chicken Alfredo. There was nothing particularly Chinese or French or Italian about these dishes, though Esther wasn't to discover that until years later, when she and Marty had money to travel.

Madame had a fondness for molded creations with an oddly anthropomorphic bent: Colonial Doll Salad (molded shrimp salad with a doll's head on top); Mock Chicken Legs (a piece of pork, wrapped in a strip of veal, to resemble a chicken leg); and Snow Man Salad (three scoops of rice, with raisin eyes and a red pimento mouth).

On the last day of class, Madame set the students loose to make Bird-of-Paradise salad, an elaborate concoction involving, among other things, fresh pineapple and a potato. Madame deftly quartered the pineapple, while the students followed along. "Careful. Careful. Careful," she chirped. "You must not cut off the top, because soon, I am going to show you a trick." But first, Madame did something with the potato, and when she was finished, she beamed. "Voila! The head. La *tête*." Finally she revealed the trick, tugging and pulling apart the leafy pineapple fronds, in a vague approximation of ruffled tail feathers.

Esther tried following suit, but pricked her finger on the pineapple leaves and had to take time out to tend to the bleeding. And hard as she tried she couldn't keep the potato from flopping off and rolling onto the floor. After the last beheading, Esther looked around the room and saw that the other students had grasped something that she had not, for she was surrounded by a covey of pineapple birds.

That afternoon, Esther slipped out of class without saying goodbye to her classmates and without, though it had been her intention, asking Madame to sign her copy of the cookbook.

And she left behind the card upon which Madame had typed the recipe du jour.

In time, Esther became a confident cook, willing to experiment with new ingredients and the latest recipes, though for years she avoided anything fancy or French.

When Ceely asks her mother why Mrs. Singh's arm is in a cast, Esther says, "It is?" She has been playing solitaire at the kitchen table and continues riffling through the deck while her daughter charges around unloading groceries. Esther, who doesn't recall asking Ceely to deliver groceries, is beginning to feel like an unwelcome guest in her own home.

"It's not hard to miss," Ceely says, as she shelves some cans.

"She's a very private woman," Esther replies, then directs Ceely to set the soup on the lower shelf. If Ceely insists on delivering groceries, despite Esther's pleas that she can buy her own, then the least she can do is store them in the right place.

Ceely slams the cans onto the lower shelf before turning to face her mother. "There's nothing private about a cast," she says.

"She fell, I think. Tripped on the hem of her sari." Esther hums as she slaps a red jack on a black queen. "That was an accident waiting to happen."

Ceely narrows her eyes at Esther. "Why don't I believe you?"

Esther recalls the young doctor's interrogation, the way he stood over Marty's bed shouting, "Marty! How many fingers do you see?" Marty's desperate eyes darted from the doctor's hand to Esther's face. She mouthed the answer, praying that he would repeat it and the doctor would proclaim him cured and send him home. But the doctor wouldn't let up. "What year is it? Who's the president? What's the date?" Finally, Esther intervened. "Please, doctor," she pleaded. "Leave him be. My husband has taken enough tests in his life."

Esther frowns at the cards, looking for a place to set the three of clubs. "Believe what you want," she says. "I didn't make the world." Then she looks up at Ceely. "Sit a minute. We'll have tea. Or coffee. I'll make a pot."

Ceely says she doesn't have time. Ceely never has time.

For a while, the two women work in silence. Then Esther says, "Mrs. Singh probably has osteoporosis."

When Ceely counters that even then, something had to cause the fracture, Esther reminds her that Helen Pearlman's fifth and sixth vertebrae snapped while she was lying in bed. "Doing nothing. Just lying there." Again, she looks up from the cards. "At that fancy place where you want to send me."

"Mrs. Singh isn't old enough to be spontaneously breaking apart." Ceely wrings out the sponge as if she were strangling it. "And I'm not sending you anywhere."

Esther sets down the cards and considers her daughter, who is now wiping the counter. She'd be prettier if she weren't so tightly wound. When had she become so overbearing, so, Esther hates to think, so insufferable? She imagines Ceely penciling sex onto the calendar.

"Listen," Esther says. "Listen to me." Surely, Ceely will listen to reason. "That place reminds me of a Holiday Inn . . . or worse, a well-appointed funeral parlor." Does Ceely really expect her to live there? Cedar Shores! Bingoville. The warehouse of the living dead. What else would you call a place where people line the lobby, slumped over in wheelchairs or staring into space? The spry ones shuffle along on canes or walkers, some with oxygen canisters trailing behind them, tubes up their noses. All the silk flowers, all the tasteful upholstery, can't disguise the stench of resignation that fills that place. The hospital where Marty died wasn't as bad.

It, at least, offered a whiff of hope, a chance for release. But nobody escapes Bingoville. No exit. No way out. No way, Jose. Esther is having none of it. For what? To ride a van to the supermarket on senior citizen Tuesdays? Attend the weekly ice cream social?

But Ceely isn't listening. "You'll have fun," she insists, as if Esther might confuse Cedar Shores with a Princess cruise to the Bahamas. Ceely is like a yappy dog, the kind that won't let go once it sinks its teeth into your calf. "I forgot! There's concierge service. Twenty-four hours a day."

"Well, I have Milo," Esther sniffs.

"Milo?" Ceely cries, in disbelief.

"Do you have a problem with Milo? Last week he fixed the toilet when it wouldn't stop running. And he has such nice manner. He takes his Cubs hat off whenever he sees me."

After Marty died, Esther worried that she relied too much on Milo. More and more she called on him to repair the things that once she might have overlooked—running toilets, clanging radiators. She enjoyed watching him work, the way he held the light-bulbs with the tips of his fingers, as if he were handling quails' eggs. She noted the way he set a faded beach towel on her kitchen floor and arranged his tools on it, before tending to the leaky faucet. He hummed while he worked, but rarely spoke. Perhaps he was reluctant to speak a language he could not command. Yet when he misappropriated verb tenses and turned simple declarative sentences into questions, Esther gently corrected him and he didn't mind. At first, Esther thought he might be Russian, but then, through the grapevine, she learned that Milo Belic, his wife Lena, and his mother, had moved to Chicago from Serbia three years ago. It was rumored that in Belgrade he had worked as a lawyer or a doctor.

Now Ceely is saying, "It's not your faucets that concern me."

"Then I don't know what you're worried about." Esther slaps

a six of hearts on a seven of diamonds. "Besides, he used to be a doctor."

"He used to be a paramedic." Ceely exaggerates the words and rolls her eyes.

"Doctor. Paramedic." Esther shrugs. "And another thing." She pauses to set a nine of spades on red hearts. "What was last Thursday about? You showed up out of the blue, hustled me into the car, and drove me to that place with the mauve napkins. You wouldn't even give me time to change."

"You looked fine, Ma."

"I suppose for a place like that, I looked fine. But nobody would have mistaken me for Zsa Zsa Gabor."

"Trust me. You looked fine. We were just going to check it out."

"Aha!" Esther slaps down an eight of diamonds. "So you admit it. You kidnapped me."

"Kidnapped?" Ceely rolls her eyes. "We had a date. Don't you remember?"

"I remember plenty. I remember staying up all night with you when you had the croup. And how about that episode in Vermont?" Esther doesn't mention the time Ceely moved back home to find herself, having had enough of that commune in Vermont. Papers and books, suede boots and turtleneck sweaters were strewn from one corner of the house to the other. For three months, Ceely camped out at the dining room table translating poems by Fernando Pessoa, a writer Esther has never understood, not even in English. But why bring all that up now?

"I won!" Esther cries, as she sets down another card. Then she sweeps up the deck and as she sets up a new game she volunteers that Mrs. Singh was mugged. "There. I hope you're satisfied."

"Satisfied?" Ceely cocks her head to one side, as if trying to make sense of a child's musings. "I wouldn't say that. But it goes to prove that the neighborhood isn't safe. You'll be much better off moving."

"Safe, schmafe," Esther says. "Now sit a minute."

Ignoring her, Ceely draws a box of All-Bran from the bag as if she'd pulled a rabbit from a hat. "Ta-da!"

Esther sighs and rolls her eyes. How many times has she told Ceely that she likes Lucky Charms. She enjoys guessing whether the sugary pellet melting on her tongue is a star, a clover, or a moon. "But this is better for you," Ceely would say, sounding like a TV commercial nobody believed.

On Mother's Day this year, Ceely gave Esther a portable phone with colossal buttons that Esther at first mistook for a toy. Ceely's gifts are like that: lights activated by the clap of a hand; a call-for-help device Esther is supposed to wear around her neck; an ergonomic can opener; a large-print edition of *Newsweek,* which Esther barely has time to read, as it takes most of the week to get through the *New Yorker.* Esther has tried explaining that her glaucoma, which is under control, does not interfere with her reading. But Ceely knows best.

Esther would prefer a silk scarf, perfume, even a box of chocolates, or that old cliché—flowers. She imagines telling Ceely that though she is old, she hasn't lost her capacity for the sensual. But then Ceely would coo, as if Esther were a child who doesn't understand that what she really wants is the whole-wheat fig bar and not the chocolate cupcake with buttercream frosting.

Ceely pours the All-Bran into Esther's favorite blue bowl, and as she slices banana on top she lectures her mother on the benefits of potassium.

Esther, who doesn't recall asking to be fed—she's already eaten—says, "I'll bear that in mind. And by the way, nice haircut."

"Thanks," Ceely says, sweeping her bangs back with a forearm.

Ceely has thick auburn hair, cut short, at odd angles. Esther once had hair like that, hair she could do something with. Then one day, she couldn't. Now every time she looks in the mirror all she can see is a woman well past her prime, with hair that resembles a collapsed soufflé.

As she sets the bowl in front of Esther, Ceely reports that her in-laws have just sold their house for over three hundred thousand dollars. "They paid eighteen for it in 1954."

"I remember when gum was a nickel," Esther says.

"You remember everything," Ceely snaps, then suddenly brightens as she seizes the opening her mother has unwittingly provided. "You remember everything," she repeats, "except where you left your purse, your glasses, and . . ." She pauses, picks up an empty bag and, skillfully as an origami master, begins pressing creases into it. "And your keys," she says, as she creates another fold.

"Oh boy," Esther mutters. Then she considers the bowl Ceely set in front of her, never mind that she'd been in the middle of a game. "First I'm moving. Now it's the keys."

"Yes, the keys," Ceely says. "We need to talk about that."

"What's there to talk about?"

"You don't want to end up on a guardrail?" Ceely's voice rises. Her speech is halting, deliberate, like Esther's when she speaks to Milo, who studies English for Newcomers at the community center. "Do you?"

Esther wishes she had a hearing aid to turn off, but despite the other infirmities of aging that plague her—glaucoma, arthritis, and slightly elevated blood pressure—her ears are in good working order. "People die when they give up the keys," she says. She picks up her spoon, eyes the cereal, and sets the spoon down. "But don't worry. I'm not driving."

"You could kill someone, Ma. Remember the man who stepped on the accelerator instead of the brakes and drove into a pedestrian mall?" Furiously, she creases the bag. "Eight people dead."

"I'm not driving," Esther lies. She looks down and considers the cereal, which even in her favorite bowl resembles kibble.

"Then sell the car. Get rid of it."

Ceely holds out her hand, as if she expects Esther to fork over the keys this very minute. Ceely is as sure of herself as Dr. Levenson. The two of them are probably in cahoots.

At her last appointment Esther could tell, by the nutty brown dome of his head, that Dr. Levenson had been somewhere warm. "You've been traveling," she'd said.

"Acapulco," he replied, as he peered into her eyes. "Next winter we're going to the Galapagos. To see the turtles. The kids are old enough now."

After switching on the light, he cleared his throat and looked down at his tasseled loafers. "Esther." He cleared his throat again, paused, and still looking down at his feet, he said, "You shouldn't be driving."

When Esther replied that she didn't drive much, and never at night, he said, "That's good. That's good." He let a few seconds pass. "But I'm talking about the daytime, too."

There he was, the picture of health, full of pronouncements and sunshine. His tan would fade soon enough, but next winter he'll swim with the turtles and acquire a fresh glow. Dr. Levenson was a good man. Still, Esther resented the assurance with which he spoke of the future. What's more, he knew nothing about her past.

The day Marty brought the car home he tooted the horn until she had to go out front and see who was making such a racket. There he was, sitting behind the wheel of a silver convertible, sporting dark glasses and a fedora. "Come on Essie." He tapped the horn in a syncopated riff. "Let's go for a spin."

He drove for miles, hugging the lakeshore, winding down

Sheridan Road, snaking through the ravines all the way to Winnetka, where he pulled into a spot overlooking the beach. After shutting the engine, he pulled her close and kissed her. Seventy-something years old, and he was taking her to a lovers' lane.

"We couldn't do this when we were teenagers, Essie."

"Who had cars?" she said, then kissed him back.

After Ceely leaves, Esther dumps the cereal into the garbage and rinses out the bowl. Then, as she crosses to the refrigerator, she imagines hearing Marty's critical voice. How many times had he warned her? "That's the first place burglars look."

It's as good as any, she thinks, as she opens the freezer door.

Yet as she reaches into the back of the freezer she pauses, afraid that her husband was right. But then her hand finds it. It's there. She pulls out the ice cream carton and sighs, satisfied that no burglar would ever think to look here.

She shuffles to the table, holding the carton as if it were filled with quails' eggs. She sets it down, pauses. Still spooked by her husband's ghost, she glances quickly over her shoulder, then chides herself for being ridiculous. Gingerly, she lifts the lid. The ring is there. A star sapphire. A gift from Marty the year he lost his way. "Men stray," her mother had said, as if she were reporting some immutable law—gravity, relativity, the orbit of the planets around the sun. Esther has never felt comfortable wearing the ring.

The pearls are there, too. She fingers the strand, recalling how they'd looked around her mother's neck, the way they rested just above the cleavage that she didn't try to conceal.

She fishes out the keys. They're cold. She wraps her hand around them and squeezes hard, relishing the feeling as they dig into her flesh. She squeezes harder, until the cold metal cuts into her, awakening her senses, like pinching herself to be sure she isn't dreaming.

One morning, while Esther is reading the obituaries, Ceely phones to say she's running out to the supermarket. "I don't need a thing," Esther says. "I'm going to the desert."

"The desert!" Ceely has a way of repeating Esther's statements as if she were pacifying a child with an overactive imagination. "The desert." She whistles.

"You'd think I just announced a trip to the moon," Esther snaps. She straightens the edges of the newspaper, which is spread out on the table before her. "I want to see the desert. Once more." Her voice trails off. "Before I die."

Ceely sighs impatiently. "You're not dying."

"Then why are you pushing me into that place?"

Impatiently, Ceely says, "It's not a dying place. And I'm not pushing you." She pauses. "It will be easier," she says, her voice softening. "That's all."

"Easier than what? Easier for whom?"

"Why do you do this?" Ceely whines, her voice rising.

"Do what?"

"Twist everything." Now she is shouting.

"Nobody lives forever," Esther declares, slapping her hand on the newspaper. Then she begins reading aloud from the obituaries, like the rabbi intoning the names of the dead before reciting the mourner's Kaddish. When she is finished, she says, "I'm off to the desert. Four nights at the Doubletree Inn. Plus a day trip to Mexico. A bus picks you up at the hotel." With each assertion, the lie blooms. Had she known how easy it was, she might have started lying sooner.

"I'm going with you," Ceely blurts.

"Maybe I don't want you to go," Esther says, quickly regretting the careless remark.

"How can you not want me to go?" Ceely is whining again, the way she did when Esther imposed a ten o'clock curfew.

"I don't need a babysitter," Esther says, sitting taller in her chair. "And besides." She pauses. "You can be unpleasant." She presses the newspaper with her hand, which is so contorted she appears to be clawing the pages. Frightened by her body's insubordination, by her inability to direct it as she wishes, she dismisses the offending hand, sending it straight to her lap. Then she hears herself saying, "Do you really want to go?" But before Ceely can reply, Esther says, "Good. Then it's settled."

Esther makes all the arrangements. She wants to visit the Desert Museum and a place where they reenact the gunfight at the O.K. Corral. She wants to ride the tram in Sabino Canyon and behold the giant saguaro. She has read about the best place for margaritas. She hopes green corn tamales will be in season. And she signs up for a day trip to Mexico.

The bus for the trip to Nogales picks them up at their hotel after breakfast. Four people have boarded by the time Ceely and Esther get on. An older couple, sporting baseball caps and fanny packs, are seated toward the front. Water bottles in mesh holders dangle from their necks. They remind Esther of the smiling couple on the Cedar Shores brochure. Seated behind them is a pair of older women who could easily be Esther and Lorraine. At the next two hotels, six more people get on, all of them considerably older than Ceely.

The driver pulls into a McDonald's parking lot about two

hundred yards from the border, and before the passengers disembark, he hands out maps of the Nogales business district. Then he holds up a map and with his finger, traces a route from the border crossing to Calle de Obregon, the street where all the pharmacies are clustered. "Hey!" The man with the water bottle interrupts. "I thought you're supposed to be our guide."

Esther elbows Ceely in the ribs and through clenched teeth whispers, "Don't make trouble." For Esther, survival has always depended on blending in, as if the next pogrom were about to sweep through the village and her only hope was to lay low. No coughing, no sneezing; not a peep until the marauders take off. This instinct is as ingrained in Esther as if she'd been born not in Chicago but in the Polish shtetl from which her parents had fled a lifetime ago. So while the rest of the group murmurs agreement with the provocateur, as the chorus of dissent swells, Esther's elbow remains firmly lodged in her daughter's ribs.

"But we signed up for a tour," the man persists.

The driver stares the group down and waving the map, says, "This is the tour. So listen up."

At the *frontera*, they push through a metal turnstile, and though Esther has traveled to Mexico many times in the past, she has never walked across the border. Entering the country is as easy as passing through a revolving door. "Mexico!" she cries triumphantly and waves her cane in the air, as if she has just circumnavigated the globe and is staking her claim to the New World.

Despite the fact that she is traveling with a cane (at Ceely's insistence), Esther leans on her daughter for support, and Ceely doesn't resist. Arm in arm they make their way along the rutted sidewalk. They pass women crouched against dusty stucco walls, clutching babies in one arm while reaching out with the other in a gesture of permanent supplication. They pass vendors selling their wares from blankets spread out on the gritty sidewalks. Other vendors carry merchandise in trays yoked around their necks with colorful woven straps. The more prosperous merchants hawk their goods from the narrow doorways of cinder-block shops. They scrape and bow, feigning respect for the women. In sing-song English, they call out, urging them to enter. "Enter!" they cry. "Take a look. Is cheaper than K-Mart."

"Don't look," Ceely whispers, pulling Esther closer.

The two women stroll past one store after another, their wares spilling out onto the sidewalk: piñatas, papier maché avocados, a lotion purportedly made from the sebaceous glands of giant sea turtles. They continue on, as if the real Nogales will present itself around the corner or on the next block. All the while, Ceely reins Esther in as the mocking cries trail after them. "How much you want to pay? How much? It's free! Lady, for you, it's free."

Suddenly Esther stops. "I think we're lost," she declares as she rummages through her straw bag for the map. She and Ceely are consulting it when a man approaches and offers to take their picture. He is short and wiry, with a pencil-thin mustache and jet-black hair slicked down and parted in the middle.

Esther looks up, smiles at him, and with an air of disbelief says, "How nice. You want to take our picture?"

"No!" Ceely cries. Then contritely, she says, "No, *gracias*," as she stalks off, pulling Esther with her.

Undeterred, the man cries out, "Real cheap!"

"*Cuanto?*" Esther calls back, as she breaks away from Ceely.

"Cheaper than K-Mart!"

"How much?" Esther holds a hand to her ear as she approaches the man, pretending she hadn't heard. By then, she is making full eye contact, as she prepares to strike a deal with the photographer.

Ceely, meanwhile, is approached by a young girl selling brilliantly colored plastic sticks that bloom from a straw basket like a bouquet of meadow flowers. The girl's creamy skin is the color of café con leche. A pink headband holds her silky black hair in place. Tiny gold earrings glint from her delicate lobes. Somebody has fussed over her. "The same somebody," Ceely later tells Esther, "who sent her into the streets to peddle plastic back-scratchers." By the time Ceely plucks a red stick from the basket, the photographer is guiding Esther onto an inverted plastic milk crate and hoisting her onto a burro.

The poor beast is dressed in a sun-bleached serape, velvet sombrero, and embroidered blinders. Despite the heat, or per-haps because of it, he stands uncomplaining, head bowed, as if hoping not to draw attention to the shame of being dressed like a caricature of a tarted-up beast of burden.

Meanwhile, his master is holding out a velvet sombrero to Esther, gesturing for her to put it on, but she shakes her head and points to her own floppy-brimmed straw hat. It is a playful hat, and together with her white linen slacks and blue striped silk blouse, Esther conveys an easy sense of style. "Hop up!" she calls to Ceely, who is standing in the distance examining her new purchase.

Ceely protests, but Esther insists, and before she knows it the man is gently pushing her up beside her mother. Then he skitters to his camera, an ancient Polaroid mounted on a tripod and cov-ered with a black cloth, giving it the air of a far more elaborate piece of equipment. He sticks his head under the cloth, then pops back out, fingers pressed to the corners of his mouth, pantomim-ing a smile. After ducking back under, he directs the women with an upheld hand and a high-pitched, syncopated whistle. "Okay!" he cries, and clicks the shutter.

As they head down the street, Esther tells Ceely she's always wanted to do that.

Bemused, Ceely says, "Have your picture taken on the back of a burro?"

"Hmmm," Esther says, dreamily.

Again, they are consulting the map, for Esther is determined to find Calle de Obregon. "Maybe we should ask someone," she is saying to Ceely, when another man approaches, this one bearing a tray of wristwatches.

"Oh, here we go again," Ceely mutters, as she tries moving her mother along.

But Esther digs in her heels. Something about the way the tray hangs from the man's neck reminds her of the long-legged girls who once moved among the tables in nightclubs, selling cigarettes and mints. Quickly seizing on Esther's hesitation, the man plucks a silver watch from his tray and holds it up till it catches the sun and glints like gaudy fishing lure.

"*No gracias*," Ceely says, as she tugs at her mother's elbow. "*No gracias*." But Esther refuses to budge.

Esther, who speaks pidgin Spanish, Spanglish, a Spanish without verbs, is nevertheless fluent in the art of the deal. She frowns and shakes her head each time the man selects a watch from his battered tray. At last she nods at a watch that looks very much like all the ones she's rejected. The man, beaming, motions for her to try it on. After great confusion over the cane, which she finally crooks over her right arm, he gently fastens the silver band around her left wrist. The two of them trade polite smiles as she holds out her arm and admires the timepiece.

Gingerly, with the help of her cane, Esther makes her way back toward Ceely, who is waiting at the end of the block. "Seiko!" she cries, waving her wrist in the air.

"Fake-o," Ceely snorts, as Esther sidles up to her.

Esther gives her daughter a baleful look. "Ten dollars. Not bad, huh?"

"Not bad," Ceely agrees.

They are walking past the duty-free shop on the Arizona side of the border when Esther says, "Let's go in."

Ceely balks and Esther, tapping her new watch, indicates they have plenty of time.

Over the years, Esther has purchased, in airport duty-free shops, Belgian chocolates, French perfumes, cloying after-dinner liqueurs. Once, at thirty thousand feet over the Atlantic, she purchased a strand of Japanese freshwater pearls. Always, upon exiting the plane, smiling flight attendants presented these purchases as if they were gifts.

Now on the American side of the border, Esther purchases a bottle of Johnnie Walker Black Label and a tube of red lipstick, but instead of being greeted by a perky flight attendant she is stopped at the door by a short, round woman dressed, not unlike a park ranger, in olive drab. Holding up her hand, the officious woman orders Esther to stop, then points to a cluster of people all clutching plastic bags similar to the one Esther is holding. "Over there," she commands. "Stand over there."

"I don't understand," Esther says.

"What don't you understand?"

"Why you want me over there."

"You want duty free?" Then she explains that Esther must re-enter Mexico, go through customs, and declare her purchases. "Then you can keep whatever is in that bag."

"But we have a bus to catch." Esther motions vaguely in the direction of the McDonald's.

The woman shrugs. "Not until you go through customs."

"But the driver." Esther's voice trails off as she points her cane to indicate where he might be. "He won't wait."

The woman, whose job it is to shepherd customers to the border where she can be sure they cross back into Mexico, in some bizarre circumvention of international law, gives Esther a withering look and again points to the group.

"Look what you've gotten us into," Ceely hisses as she pulls her mother aside.

In a voice intended to carry, Esther says, "She won't listen to reason." Glaring at the woman, she tells Ceely, "Nobody said anything about returning to Mexico. It's the most ridiculous thing I've ever heard."

"You didn't think you'd get duty free for nothing?"

"You sound like my father," Esther frowns. "No lunch is for free, Esther. How many times did I hear that?"

"Well, Poppy had a point."

A point? What was the point? That Esther wasn't good enough, deserving enough of life's little perks? It occurs to her now, as she clutches the bag, that she's gone through life saying no thank you to second helpings, and denying herself all the trimmings. Others got the drumstick, the cherry on the sundae, while Esther politely held back, lest she be accused of trying to get something for nothing.

Vexed, Esther says, "Please, Ceely. Don't start with me."

"I shouldn't start? You're the one who got us into this. Now we're going to miss the bus." With a nod toward the woman, Ceely says, "You realize, she hates us."

"Don't be ridiculous!"

"She does. You can tell," Ceely insists. "She thinks we're greedy Americans. Stupid gringos."

"How do you know what she thinks?"

"Besides, how many bargains do you need?" Ceely rattles a bag full of purchases Esther made after lunch: Prozac, Ambien, Lipitor, Retin-A, Trusopt, Valium. She complains that Esther had tricked her into going on a drug run. "You told me you wanted to see the desert."

"I do. I did. We did," Esther insists. "What do you think we drove through on the bus?"

Ceely gives her mother a baleful look and Esther lectures her daughter on the perfidies of the drug companies. "Big Pharma," she says. "Big Pharma keeps prices so high that people cut their prescriptions in half or go without food to pay for their drugs. Big Pharma lies about clinical trials, suppressing questionable results."

"You're beginning to sound like a talk radio nut," Ceely says.

"And the government's in on it," Esther says, with finality.

"But you don't even take these," Ceely says.

"Some are for gifts."

"Gifts?" Ceely moans.

"Look!" Esther cries. "Look who's here."

"Please don't change the subject," Ceely whines.

"The couple." Esther points with her cane. "From the bus." Leaning closer, she whispers, "The ones with the water bottles. Over there, by the Swiss Army knives. Wouldn't you know it." She waves her cane again. "Hello," she calls from across the aisle.

They smile and wave back.

"I would have figured you have plenty of those already," Esther cries out.

"Christmas presents." The man beams.

"What a great idea. But remember not to take them on the

plane. My daughter had one confiscated at security," Esther says, nodding toward Ceely. "They called it contraband. Contraband! Can you believe it? She looks like a terrorist, don't you agree?"

"Ma," Ceely tugs at Esther's sleeve. "You're shouting."

"Oh, what difference does it make?" Esther pulls away.

Then it's Ceely's turn to point and exclaim. "Look! They're leaving."

The woman masquerading as a park ranger is addressing the group.

"Then get going." Esther takes the drugs from Ceely, trading them for the bag with the lipstick and the scotch. Gently, she pushes her daughter toward the group.

Ceely looks confused. "What do you expect me to do with these?"

"You'll go."

"Where?"

"With the woman."

"The coyote?" Ceely snorts. "She isn't sneaking me across the border. These are yours." She tries pushing the bag back into Esther's hands, but Esther resists. "You're making a scene," she hisses.

"I'm not going." Ceely sounds petulant, like the three-year-old who'd stomped her foot whenever she didn't get her way.

"Get going," Esther says, nudging Ceely gently toward the group.

"But we'll miss the bus," Ceely cries.

"Don't be ridiculous." Again Esther taps her watch. "We have plenty of time."

"But you don't even drink," Ceely argues, holding up the bottle of scotch.

"I like to have something on hand. You never know who will stop by. Maybe Mrs. Singh. Or that nice neighbor upstairs.

Mr. Volz. Now do your old mother a favor," Esther says, again pushing Ceely toward the departing group.

Ceely is disappearing across the store when Esther cries, "Wait!"

Ceely turns and stops, a look of concern crossing her face. "What? What's wrong?"

"Nothing," Esther says. She scurries as fast as she can to her daughter's side and kisses her on the cheek, the way she had on Ceely's very first day of school. Then she pats her arm and says, "Get going, or you'll be late."

At dinner, over margaritas, the two women recount their day. Esther holds out her arm, admiring the watch, and Ceely agrees that it's a good imitation. Then Esther says, "I almost forgot! The picture." She pulls it out of her handbag and sets it on the table between them.

"Look at me," Ceely says. "I'm so stiff. Why can't I ever take a good picture?" She pauses, searching her mother's eyes for the truth. "Or maybe it's my true visage?"

"Nobody looks good on a donkey," Esther insists. "Look at me. I'm not even facing the camera."

It's true. Esther, who has always been a substantial presence, full-figured when women were admired for being zaftig, as Marty called her, appears shrunken in the photo, like a garment tossed in the wash on the wrong cycle. She's looking away, off into the distance, as if something has caught her by surprise. Later, Ceely will study the picture, show it to Lorraine and wonder if she'd missed some early warning sign. "I don't know what it is," she will tell Lorraine.

Perhaps, she will think, it's the effect of the floppy-brimmed hat, or the fact that Esther had turned just as the shutter clicked, but her mother appears in shadow, as if she is not fully present, as if she has chosen to hop on that tired beast to begin her journey to the other side.

Lately when Esther opens her eyes, she can't remember if there is a reason to get out of bed. Sometimes, in the attenuated morning light, she mistakes the chest of drawers for Marty. She has seen her mother in the clothes she sets out on the rocker before bedtime. And then her eyes might wander to the crack in the ceiling, which in her dreamy, fugue state resembles a line snaking across a map. The Mississippi River, or the less commanding Chicago. When she discovered the crack, in the inconsolable days after Marty died, it had felt like a metaphor for her fractured life.

She's been meaning to tell Milo about it, see if it is something that he can fix. Then she forgets. Besides, the crack is useful, not unlike the grid on that chart Dr. Levenson gave her. His nurse taught Esther to stare at the dot in the grid's center, first with one eye, then the other. "Call," she said, "if the lines get wavy."

Some mornings, Esther recalls the old days when the radio jarred her awake. Marty kept it tuned to traffic updates; she listened for the weather, to know how to dress the children for school. The two of them would lie there taking in the headlines, before rushing headlong into the day. The news was as bad then as now. Vietnam. Protests. Race riots. Assassinations—one after the other. Once, rioters destroyed a three-mile stretch of Chicago's West Side. Those were terrible times. These are bad times, too, maybe worse since it feels as if nobody cares. Certainly nobody protests, though there's plenty of cause for that. At times, Esther imagines a collective shrug passing over the nation. A dull complacency has taken hold. Perhaps nations have life spans. Like birds. Dogs. People. "And ours is in the last throes," she says, staring up at the ceiling. "Just like me."

The crack. She's already decided that the day she can't see it is the day she'll call Ceely. "Come and get me," she'll say. "You can put me in that place now." Today, though, even without her glasses, she can make out the wavering line. "It's still here," she whispers. "And so am I."

The fact of her existence, of waking and breathing and going through the motions of another day, of being Esther, does not so much surprise her as give her pause. Lately, though she is not a believer, she's taken to murmuring a plea at bedtime to whatever merciful force might listen—Yahweh, Allah, God, Adonai. Let me die before I wake. Sometimes, she edits the prayer, attaching certain conditions to her entreaty. If tomorrow is the day I paint my eyebrows with lipstick, then please let me die.

It's the dementia that she fears the most. Recently, she broached the matter with Lenny, her son-in-law, the expert on aging. She'd tried sounding curious and bright, as if she might be preparing to write a dissertation on the topic; not doing research on her own behalf. "Is there a point," she asked, "when you know you are about to cross over?" Then she told Lenny about Helen painting her eyebrows with lipstick. "One day she's applying color to her lips, the next, boom!" She paused. "My question is, do you know?"

"Know?" He raked a hand through his wiry hair and considered her through enormous Coke-bottle lenses, as if she were speaking a language he did not understand.

She nodded. "Do you know when you're about to do something like that, like putting lipstick on your forehead? There must be a, what do they call it, you know, a tipping point?"

"The beginning of the end?" He gazed at her intently.

"Yes," she muttered, quickly looking down, afraid that he could read her mind, that he had surmised she was, after all, making inquiries on her own behalf.

"Well, I don't know, Esther. I think it's more gradual than that. Incremental. But you know, dementia isn't my area of expertise."

She should have known that was coming. Everybody's a specialist. Even Dr. Levenson. Recently, when he finished checking her eyes, she mentioned that her feet appeared more swollen than usual. He shrugged and said he was sorry to hear that, but he didn't know anything about feet. But you're a doctor, she'd wanted to say. At some point, you studied the body, head to toe.

And Lenny, the noted expert on aging, couldn't tell her if she'll wake up one morning as someone other than the woman who'd set her head on the pillow the night before. So Esther resorts to a higher power, to some force that might see to it that she exits this life without disgracing herself.

She has spent a lifetime striking bargains with God. As a young woman, on the chance that some higher power might be listening, Esther, a hypochondriac prone to thinking that she had one fatal disease or another, would close her eyes and pray. Please let me live to Barry's bar mitzvah. Then you can kill me. She sought numerous reprieves. Let me live until Ceely graduates from high school. Then she wanted to dance at her daughter's wedding, hold her first grandchild, pass the Torah at her grandson's bar mitzvah.

Esther's deathday became a moving target.

Now Barry, the hotshot dentist with the fancy North Shore practice, is in financial trouble, and Ceely and Lenny are in couple's therapy. All Esther ever wanted was to shepherd her children into self-sufficiency. She never wanted to live to see them fall apart. And she certainly doesn't want to lose her marbles before taking her last breath.

And so she's begun to beseech a higher power. Yahweh, Allah, God, Adonai. Let me die before I wake. Or at least let me collapse on an Oriental carpet like Jimmy Pearlman.

One minute, Helen's husband was paying bills at his desk, the next he was keeled over on a silk prayer rug. There are worse ways to exit. She could die like Marty, with a young doctor waving his fingers in her face. Or she could take her last breath in that place where Ceely wants to put her.

Suddenly, Esther hears Mr. Volz padding around upstairs, starting his day. On occasion she sees young men trailing after him up the stairs. She listens now for an extra set of footsteps, but today it is only Timothy Volz. Odd, how familiar she's become with his habits, yet how little she really knows about him. Like a husband. How well had she known Marty after fifty years, after all those mornings in bed listening to the radio?

In a few minutes, water will whoosh through Mr. Volz's pipes. In twenty, his door will close and he'll make his way down the stairs past Esther's apartment. Then she'll hear the vestibule door bang shut, the slam of a taxi door, the crush of gravel on asphalt as his cab pulls away.

"A regular Rockefeller," her sister-in-law called him, after Esther reported that her neighbor rode taxis everywhere. Clara, who never learned to drive, was too nervous in taxis, always watching the meter, suspecting the driver of taking the longest route. If Harry couldn't drive her, Clara took a bus. Lately, that loopy Fanny Pearlman, Helen's daughter, had been carting Clara around to doctors' appointments, the hairdresser, even all the way to Highland Park to visit her son and his uptight wife.

The bedroom window vibrates as a garbage truck rumbles by. The day has begun; people have places to go, things to do. Even the autistic boy who lives across the courtyard next to Lorraine has started to practice. Esther can hear the music. Every morning he plays a haunting medley. It segues from something by Erik Satie, to "Eleanor Rigby," and finally to the theme song from *Cheers*. Whenever he gets to that last part, a feeling, something like longing, comes over Esther, though she can't say for what. Her life, she supposes. Not that she'd care to repeat it all, though she certainly isn't greedy enough to cherry-pick only the good parts. She longs for just an ordinary morning with Marty at her side, listening to the news, the weather, the traffic updates, a morning when she doesn't wake and wonder if today is the day when her body finally succumbs, overtakes her, the day when she falls and breaks a hip, has a stroke, or worse, loses her marbles before her heart stops beating.

She reaches for her glasses on the nightstand but stays in bed, politely waiting for the music to end. The boy plays the medley three times without stopping. Every day, the same routine. Now he's starting at the top. These kids get in a rut. Can't help it. Esther is in a rut, too. Every day, the same. Look for the crack. Strike bargains with God. But then she'll find herself listening to the footsteps, the rush of water, the taxi pulling away. And she'll find herself waiting for the music.

When the music ends, a brilliant chirping erupts from the living room, as if the bird, too, has been waiting politely to start its day.

It is time to get up, go into the living room, lift the pillowcase off the cage, change the water, fill the seed dish, line the cage with yesterday's newspaper. Then Esther will wait for Lorraine's call and make up the rest of the day as she goes along.

Esther is at the kitchen table, nursing a mug of tea and going through the newspaper while waiting for Lorraine to call. Always, she starts with the obituaries, then works her way through the rest of the bad news—war, famine, the endless terror of the human condition. She ends on a lighter note with Ann Landers and the funnies. On the really bad news days, she'll turn to the sports, especially when the Cubs are playing. Then she can commiserate with Milo, an avid fan, over something other than the weather.

She didn't always start with the obituaries, and can even recall a time when she scanned them with a kind of detachment, as if the subject at hand did not apply to her. Not that she ever assumed she would be the one to get a free pass. Yet reading the notices as she once did, Marty seated across from her at the kitchen table, the sugar bowl and vitamins on a doily between them, her coffee mug set squarely on a blue quilted placemat, death was something remote, something that happened to other people.

Then Marty died.

Esther recalls the week after his funeral when she opened the morning paper and, in her grief, had mistaken it for that day's edition. As was her habit, she turned first to the obituaries. Her trained eye scanned the names, barely reading them, for in a city as large as Chicago, Esther could go weeks without knowing any of the deceased. Most days her eye fixed only on the number beside the name, where upon a quick actuarial accounting she understood that she had, by almost any measure, already beaten the odds.

But that morning after Marty's funeral her eye tripped and stumbled on a bold block of type. Then came the shock of recognition. Lustig, Martin.

L-u-s-t-i-g. M-a-r-t-i-n. She decoded the letters, stringing them together, like a child learning to read. Then her name jumped out and her mouth went dry. What was she doing there, her name nestled among the dead? It felt like a sneak preview, a coming attraction for the day when she would boldly appear, and the names of her children, grandchildren, the husband who had predeceased her, would traipse faintly behind. Perhaps someone would think to add a personal touch, though nobody had thought of doing that for Marty.

The woman whose name appeared below Marty's was remembered for the stuffed mushrooms and the laughter she brought to family gatherings. Her name was Lenore. Esther wondered about Lenore's laugh. Esther's friend Helen, a smoker, laughed until the phlegm rattled in her chest. Her mother had snorted when she laughed. Her son doesn't know how to laugh. Whenever Esther says something funny, Barry smiles, and even then, only one side of his mouth turns up. Even his smile is crooked. She imagined Lenore's laughter sounded like wind chimes in a gentle breeze.

Sharing the page with Lenore and Marty was a man who had organized family reunions every July for twenty-three years. And there was a woman who'd worn fanciful hats. Esther's hats were on hooks in the front hall closet, but were any of them fanciful? Had she ever organized a reunion? For a few years, when the children were younger, she sang in the temple choir. She couldn't remember why she ever quit.

Esther's favorite was the woman who didn't take "no" for an answer. When Esther was mad at Marty, she'd purse her lips and sometimes leave the room to cry into a stack of towels. Then she'd come round to whatever point of view he wished her to adopt. She'd never stood up to Lustig, Martin. Not that she hadn't tried, but when Marty said, "No," Esther eventually caved in.

Ordinary. Perhaps that's how they'd describe Esther, which was how Miss Smaller in 3G had been remembered in her obituary. Poor Miss Smaller. If a body didn't decompose, give off a stench worse than rotten potatoes, how long until anyone would have missed her? Milo discovered her body. A heart attack. She was young for that. Midfifties. But a heart attack, all the same. For days, nobody claimed the body. Finally, a phone number on a slip of paper led to a niece, the one who posted the obituary. "Miss Smaller was an ordinary woman," it said. There was mention of a brief marriage; a son, killed by a drunk driver. For eighteen years she'd managed the makeup counter at a pharmacy on Diversey. Milo told Esther that Miss Smaller rode the bus to work every day at the same time. Esther regretted never talking to the woman, but if they passed on the sidewalk, Miss Smaller always looked away.

Esther hoped Miss Smaller flickered across the bus driver's mind when he passed her stop. Perhaps her coworkers phoned, and perhaps somebody even suggested checking on her. But people get busy. It's possible Miss Smaller had talked at work about moving to Arizona, Florida, someplace warm, and everyone assumed she'd finally gone ahead and done it. No need to give notice. Not for a job like that, standing behind a counter selling lipstick and cheap perfume. For days, her body lay undiscovered.

At least Esther doesn't have to worry about that. She and Lorraine have their system. The day she doesn't answer, Lorraine will call for help. There will be no time for the foul stench of death to betray her. She will exit neatly, quietly. But what if Lorraine goes first? Had they ever considered the fate of the one who will be left behind? She slaps her forehead, laughing in disbelief.

Even after Miss Smaller's death, Esther and Lorraine hadn't considered the flaw in their plan. Instead, Lorraine had asked Esther, "What would you say about me?"

They were sitting in the courtyard, beside the statue of Saint Francis. "Say?" Esther looked quizzically at her friend.

"You know. After I'm gone."

Esther glared at her friend. "What kind of question is that?"

She and Lorraine had known each other since high school. What was there to say? Since retiring, Lorraine had been studying Italian and serving meals to the homeless. She'd roped Esther into a writing class at the community center. She baked elaborate birthday cakes for her nieces, and hazelnut tortes for special occasions. "Well," Esther hesitated. "I would say . . . I suppose I would say. I would say that you don't share your recipes."

Lorraine's face collapsed. "This isn't the time for jokes."

Later, Esther phoned her friend and apologized. "The truth is, you do so much, Lorraine, that I didn't know where to begin. But should anyone ask, I'd have to say, 'She made the most spectacular hazelnut tortes.'"

Now, waiting for her friend to call, Esther looks up from the obituaries and sees, as if for the first time, the vitamins, the sugar bowl, the ruffled edging on the blue quilted placemat. Such homely objects. Yet each has a sense of purpose. The longer she stares at them, the more they mock her with their specificity. They know what they're about. They aren't sitting around, conjuring the few taglines that might explain the meaning of their existence.

Esther looks forward to Tuesdays, the day she and Lorraine go to the community center for "Brown Bag Journaling."

She supposes the class is scheduled at the noon hour to give busy people the opportunity to sandwich one more activity into their day. But the idea of eating and writing at the same time doesn't appeal to her. Multitasking, they call it; Esther calls it rude. It used to be you'd pay to see someone eating fire while walking a tightrope. Now people walk or drive or stand in the checkout line at the Jewel while talking on the phone, checking e-mail, or plugging music into their ears. They text messages while shifting lanes on the Edens Expressway. The other day, Sophie kept checking her cell phone while she and Esther were having tea.

The truth is Esther manages to arrange her activities sequentially and still have time to spare. Yet the irony is how quickly time is running out.

The class was Lorraine's idea. At first, Esther resisted, declaring, "I'm not a writer."

"You'll learn," Lorraine countered.

Dubiously, Esther shook her head. She's never kept a diary. She's never even been surveyed to state her choice in a presidential race (unconditional Democrat), or to say whether or not she favors riverboat gambling (she does not), or whether she believes in global warming (as if that were a matter of faith). Until five years ago, Esther had been Marty's wife. Now she is a widow.

"I'm too old to learn," Esther said.

"It's therapeutic," Lorraine insisted.

"Says who?" Esther asked with annoyance. "Dr. Phil?"

Since Lorraine retired as a legal secretary she's become an aficionado of daytime TV. Oprah. Judge Judy. She quotes them all. After Marty died, she gave Esther a notebook. "It's to write down your feelings," she said.

Though Esther isn't convinced of the remedial powers of writing, she agreed to the journaling class when Lorraine said, "If you don't get out more, that daughter of yours is going to put you in assisted living. You'll be playing bingo instead of writing stories."

Now Esther finds herself seated in a classroom that was last decorated by a teacher who'd taken Black History Month to heart. Fraying pictures of Martin Luther King and Rosa Parks are taped to the cinder-block wall. A faded copy of the "Dream" speech is tacked to a crumbling bulletin board. The students are gathered around a large round table, with the teacher, a young thing Esther mistook for another student on the first day, democratically positioned in their midst. She is instructing them to close their eyes. "You're six years old," she says, her voice soft, hypnotic. "You're in your mother's kitchen. What do you see?" She wants details. Smells. Colors. Sounds. Every little knickknack.

When Esther closes her eyes all she can see is the tattoo on the teacher's wrist, the severe eyeglasses that mask a pretty face. She must be Sophie's age, twenty-five, maybe twenty-eight. I dare you to try this when you're eighty-five, Esther wants to say. Try conjuring a kitchen you haven't thought about in decades.

Then out of nowhere, a faded yellow linoleum floor appears, along with a round oak table and four mismatched chairs. Her mother is on hands and knees scrubbing the floor. The room smells of coffee and Spic and Span. Then Esther sees a pink cut-glass bowl filled with fruit. Her father is sitting at the kitchen table after dinner sipping hot tea from a tall glass and peeling the skin off an apple with a pearl-handled knife. The peel falls away in one long, continuous swirl.

After class, Esther and Lorraine head to Wing Yee's and settle into their favorite booth, the one that flanks the window but still affords a clear view of the fish tank at the far end of the room. After the waitress sets down two cups and a pot of tea, Lorraine glances around the room then back at Esther and says, "Why are we here?"

"What are you talking about?" Esther's voice wavers between irritation and concern. "We come here every week."

"I know, I know. But maybe we should have brought our lunch, like the others." She asks if Esther noticed that the woman in the pink sweatshirt brought an apple, a sandwich, three Fig Newtons, and a bottle of water. "Even the anorexic next to me brought something," Lorraine says.

Esther, who had taken stock of all the lunches, shakes her head and asks Lorraine which she'd prefer, "Carrot sticks and a carton of yogurt, or chicken chow mein with fried rice?"

"But people will think we're standoffish," Lorraine says.

"Let them." Esther shoots her friend a baleful look. "We're both eighty-five years old. We can do as we please."

"I suppose you're right," Lorraine sighs, as she slips her chopsticks out of their paper wrapper. "Still."

"Still, nothing. Now tell me what you wrote."

"Not much," Lorraine confesses. "I could see my mother peeling potatoes at the kitchen sink. She was wearing a full apron over a housedress. There was a yellow clock above the stove that had stopped telling time at 7:25. My mother never fixed it. I don't know why. It never even occurred to me that she could fix it. Or get a new one. Funny, what comes back. Seven twenty-five. After all these years."

The waitress brings their order and Lorraine fills their cups with jasmine tea. "How about you?"

Esther describes the smell of detergent, the sight of her father peeling an apple. "That all came back. But honestly, Lorraine." She pauses, not sure how to express an uneasy feeling that's taken hold of her. "Honestly, I think it's easier to predict the future than to remember the past."

Lorraine arches a perfectly plucked eyebrow, waiting for Esther to explain. This would be how she looked taking dictation, steno pad propped in her lap, pencil poised, waiting on Mr. Stein's every word. Like now, her lipstick would have been perfect; every silver-blond hair would have known its place.

"The problem," Esther continues, "is that my future is too predictable." She asks if Lorraine remembers the ads that promised no surprises at Holiday Inn. "Somehow, knowing exactly what to expect, before you arrived, was supposed to be comforting. What I'm trying to say is that I'd delight in a bit of surprise. Today, for example, I knew before we sat down that you would order the chicken chow mein with fried rice, and I would order the vegetable egg foo young, and that we would exclaim, when our plates arrived, that next time we'll branch out and try something new." She runs a fork through her food, as if it might present itself as something different. Then she sets her fork down and sinks back into the booth. "Even before we arrived, I could see us sitting here by the window, with you facing the fish tank because it was your turn for that, and we'd be bickering all the way to the arrival of the fortune cookies."

Lorraine grips a piece of chicken between the pincers of her chopsticks (which she can manage, unlike Esther, whose hands are too hobbled by arthritis). Slowly, she brings it to her mouth and chews. At last, she looks over at Esther and says, "When was the last time you stayed at a Holiday Inn?"

Esther laughs, then, realizing that Lorraine isn't joking, glares at her friend and asks, "How's the chow mein?"

Finally, Esther allows that she saw her mother on her hands and knees scrubbing the kitchen floor. And from there she'd conjured a kitchen in the Indiana Dunes. "The rich families drove to Wisconsin, to Lake Geneva, to the fancy resorts. But we spent two weeks every summer at Mrs. Zaretsky's rooming house in the Dunes. Four or five families crowded into her home, one family to a room. The men stayed in the city during the week, leaving the women and children to enjoy the fresh air and the beach. I loved the commotion, the sound of the screen door slamming, the cries of the children playing tag. And then Mrs. Zaretsky would come tearing out and yell at us to pipe down and stay away from her flowers. At any time of day, you could find a couple of women in the kitchen. Someone was always complaining that somebody, she's not naming names because that somebody knows who she is, took two eggs from her shelf in the refrigerator." Esther pauses and stares out the window, as if those summer days were parading past the plate glass window.

"Go on," Lorraine urges.

"Where was I?"

"Someone had taken the eggs."

"Right! The eggs. But by the end of the day, when the cooking was done and the children had been fed, the women sat around the table gossiping, as if they hadn't spent the afternoon trading insults and accusations. I loved crouching in a corner, listening to their stories. Sooner or later, though, someone would point a finger and say, 'How long has she been there?'"

Esther closes her eyes and smiles. When she opens them, she says, "They called those summer places *kachaleyns*. It means 'cook alone.' Funny, because nobody was ever alone in that kitchen." She shrugs. "I suppose the name was meant to be ironic."

The next day, while waiting for Lorraine's call, Esther takes out her journal and reads the entry in which her mother is washing the floor. "You and your floors," she says, smiling, as if her mother were sitting right beside her. If only she could have smiled when her mother was alive. Oh, how they fought. Was there anything that didn't trigger a quarrel? Even her mother's obsession with floors became grist for Esther's anger.

Esther can still hear the pride in her mother's voice as she pronounced, about one woman or another, "Her floors are so clean, you can eat off them." This bestowing of praise for cleanliness, as if it were really a virtue, drove Esther, whose housekeeping standards were rather lax, berserk. Once, after Esther's mother had sung a song of praise for her daughter-in-law Clara's floors, Esther set Barry in the middle of her mother's kitchen with a can of PLAY-DOH and told the toddler, "Make Nonna a cake." When Mrs. Glass protested that she'd just washed the floor, Esther reached into her bag and handed the toddler another can of clay. At this, Mrs. Glass collapsed onto the nearest chair, opened the top three buttons of her housedress, fanned herself with her hand and waited for her dizzy spell to pass.

Now Esther makes a fresh entry in her journal. "I'm sorry," she writes, then studies the words. Is this what the teacher had in mind when she instructed the class to write something every day? "Even one line," she'd said, explaining how one sentence often leads to another. Esther ponders the entry, wondering whether two words constitute a sentence. And suddenly she is writing more, her thoughts tumbling faster than she can transfer them onto the page. You were right, Ma. About so many things. Not about the floors. You and I will never agree on that, though you'll be pleased to know that my standards, though nothing like Clara's, have improved. Yet I think I understand. When you got down on your hands and knees and ran that sudsy rag across the linoleum, you were in command. You ruled from that homely room with the noisy refrigerator and the dripping faucet. You were safe there in a way you never were in the world outside the home. When you stepped outside you might get lost, and when you spoke, the only words you uttered in frustration might be in Yiddish. Then who would understand you, help you find your way back home? Even after you'd been here for more years than you'd lived there, in that place you had to flee, you felt safer in your kitchen, scrubbing the floor until it sparkled. You were safe, and by extension, so were we. This was your way of making us feel protected.

Esther sets down her pen and wonders if Ceely will ever sit like this and wish things had been otherwise. Perhaps she should warn her daughter. "Let's talk. Now. Before it's too late." But Ceely is too busy, even for a cup of coffee.

Esther runs her hand over the page, over the image of her mother on hands and knees, vigorously shaping her world. Then she picks up her pen and absentmindedly starts listing all of the other kitchens she's inhabited, stopping when she reaches the room in the house where she and Marty had started their days over ever so many cups of coffee.

On one such morning Esther recalls setting a plate of rye toast beside Marty's orange juice before trying to tell him about a dream. Though most of her dreams got away quicker than those thousand-legged bugs that scurry down the bathtub drain before she could catch them, she couldn't shake this one.

Marty, who had been reading the morning paper, looked up and regarded her as if he might be considering the implications of her dream. Esther, meanwhile, bustled about the kitchen, waiting for her husband's reply. She waited while he ate a slice of toast, wiped his mouth, and carefully set the napkin back on his lap. She waited while he buttered a second toast triangle. As he reached for the jam, she could no longer contain herself. "It was the strangest dream," she confessed.

He set down the knife, picked up his cup, took a sip of coffee, and nodded, as if pondering his reply. With great deliberation, he returned the cup to its saucer. Finally, he said, "Do I look like Dr. Freud?"

Marty looked nothing like the distinguished headshrinker. Dr. Freud was a regular mensch, with that lean, intelligent face and neatly cropped beard. Marty's face was round as the beets Esther boiled for borscht, and when he was angry, it turned just as red.

At last, satisfied that he needed nothing else, Esther sat down. She considered the toast, which had turned stone cold. She straightened her place mat. She picked up her juice glass and set it down again, as she struggled to speak to her husband, who was skimming the sports page. When she could no longer hold her tongue, she said, "What's the matter with you, Marty? Why are you always so angry?"

He turned the page and without looking up, muttered, "What do you want from me, Esther?"

"Nothing," she sighed, as she plucked a slice of cold toast from the basket.

But it wasn't nothing. In her dream, Ceely was a child again, sitting at the kitchen table cutting hearts out of red paper and doilies while Esther put the finishing touches on dinner. Glitter, which Ceely sprinkled on the valentines, the way Esther dusted sugar on the tops of poppyseed cookies, had caught like fairy dust in the dimples of her rosy cheeks and in the folds of her thick, auburn braids. Ceely was wearing a yellow cardigan with a starched white Peter Pan collar peeking out at the neckline. Esther, overcome by this angelic vision, wiped her hands on her apron, floated across the table and wrapped her arms around the child. She pressed her face into Ceely's braids, which smelled of Breck shampoo and Elmer's glue. She nuzzled deeper, inhaling huge gulps of the child's sweetness. Suddenly, she was sailing through the air and when she landed, her head hit the stove. Esther opened her eyes and saw Ceely standing over her, all in black, from the tips of her dyed hair to the toes of her steel-tipped boots. "I told you to stay away!" Ceely shrieked. Then she stormed out of the kitchen, leaving a trail of scuff marks on the freshly waxed floor. A few minutes later she returned, her arms piled with garments that Esther had sewn over the years: party dresses with smocking across the bodice; plaid schoolgirl jumpers; pleated skirts; seersucker rompers. She dropped the pile at Esther's feet, then stomped on it and hissed, "Return to sender."

"But I thought you liked them!" Esther cried.

Esther didn't need Marty, sitting there with the newspaper, or Dr. Freud, to tell her that the clothes in her dream represented the many letters that Ceely had been returning unopened. Esther would never forget the first one—a red envelope stuck between the junk and the bills—and her excitement at being the recipient of such an intriguing piece of mail. Then she saw that the letter was addressed to Ceely, and next to the address, scrawled in Ceely's loopy script: Return to Sender. Thinking there must be some mistake, Esther stuck the valentine into a fresh envelope, along with a ten-dollar bill and a note to buy something special.

When that envelope came back, too, Esther marched to the phone and in the middle of the day dialed long distance, as if she were the president of AT&T. A cheerful voice on the other end announced that Ceely wasn't in. "But I'll tell her you called." It was always a different cheery voice. Ceely is at work. Ceely went to a movie. Ceely just ran out for a carton of milk. They all promised to inform Ceely that Esther had called.

In the beginning, Marty refused to get involved. "Leave her alone. She's busy."

But Esther stood her ground. "Too busy to return a call? Too busy to talk for five minutes? I even told the girl . . . listen to me, I don't even know the girl's name. We don't know who Ceely is living with. I told the girl, 'Have Ceely call collect.'" Esther paused to catch her breath, then pleading, said, "What's the matter with you, Marty? She's eighteen years old. She can pick up a phone."

Six months later, Ceely wrote and told them to stop trying to make contact. There was no return address on the envelope, only a faded postmark from Vermont.

It was Marty's idea to search for Ceely.

Esther, who had been chopping onions for a mushroom barley soup when he announced his plan, put down the knife and turned to face her husband. "Vermont's a big place," she said.

"We'll hire someone. He'll find out what's what."

"Who, Marty? Who are we going to hire?"

"A detective."

"This isn't like the movies," she said, turning back to her work.

A few minutes later Marty plunked a phone book on the kitchen table. "Take a look," he said.

Esther wiped her hands on her apron as she shuffled to the table. "What is it, Marty?" she sighed. "I don't have time for games."

"Look," he said, jabbing a yellow page with his stubby finger. "It says here, 'Private Investigators.' There's an entire page of them. See for yourself. We're not alone, Esther. There must be lots of people like us. People looking for somebody."

Silently, she returned to the chopping board. As she set to work on a carrot, which, through her tears, resembled her husband's thick finger, she wondered what kind of heartbreak all those other homebodies might have caused.

Three weeks later, Esther and Marty were seated on hard wooden chairs, staring across a cluttered desk at Jack Kolner, the detective they'd picked from the Yellow Pages because Esther liked the sound of his name.

When Jack reported that he'd found Ceely and she'd threatened him with a knife, Marty's face turned so red that Esther thought her husband was having a stroke. She reached over and stroked his hand, but Marty, ignoring her touch, leaped from his chair and shook his fists at the ceiling. Then Jack was on his feet waving him back down and speaking in reassuring tones. "That sort of thing happens in this line of work," he said. But Jack didn't strike Esther as the sort who was accustomed to having knives pulled on him. He wasn't much younger than Marty; a little old to be running around spying on people.

After Marty calmed down, Jack tried to assure them. "It was one of those Swiss Army knives. And it wasn't open." He paused. "I suppose I should have been clearer about that." Then he informed them that Ceely was living on a commune outside of Burlington.

"Commune?" Marty and Esther sounded confused, so Jack explained that everyone pitched in as best they could to help support the group.

Esther, annoyed, said, "I know about communes. I just didn't think Ceely was that kind of girl."

Jack informed them that Ceely was making pottery, which she sold at street fairs in the summer.

"And in the winter?" Marty asked.

"Shush, Marty. Let the man speak," Esther said, patting her husband's hand.

But Jack didn't have much more to say. He tipped back in his chair and rolled two steel balls in the palm of his hand, as if it were now Marty and Esther's turn to offer some vital piece of information.

Before leaving, they asked Jack to find out more. Anything. How was Ceely's health? Was there a boyfriend, perhaps? Did she have enough money?

Three weeks later, they received a letter from Ceely. She was aware that they had hired someone to snoop on her. She threatened to sue them.

That's when Marty announced that as far as he was concerned Ceely was dead, and for the next week he sat shiva for their daughter.

Esther still remembered the way Marty's hand shook as he phoned Greenberg, his assistant, and told him to look after the store for a few days. "I'm fine, Abe. No. Just a little vacation."

Then, in accordance with tradition, Marty lit a candle, covered the mirrors with pillowcases, ripped his best shirt in the spot opposite his heart, stopped shaving, and for the next seven days moped around the house in worn slippers, mourning the death of a daughter who was very much alive—in Vermont. Meanwhile, Esther went about her business with pursed lips, steering clear of her husband as she made the bed, dusted, prepared dinner as always. She played solitaire and sewed new curtains for the kitchen. She finished the book that had been on her nightstand for weeks, and read the newspaper from cover to cover.

Sometime during that morose week, Esther cut an ad from the paper. Someone was seeking an apartment sitter. Though she didn't feel qualified for much, Esther figured she had the skills to look after a home. For the rest of the week, while Marty moped, the ad rolled around in her mind like the butterscotch candies she sucked on while doing the housework.

Esther waited until Marty returned to work before calling to inquire about 1 BR near shops and el. Lots of light. She let the phone ring three times before hanging up and tucking the ad away in her jewelry box. She could go weeks without thinking about it. Then something would happen—like the morning Marty stormed off before breakfast because he couldn't find his argyle socks—and she'd remember the ad, nestled beneath her mother's pearls and the Lady Bulova that Marty had given her on her fortieth birthday.

On those occasions when Esther started to dial the number, she'd remind herself that nobody in her family had ever left, not until death did them part. And then she'd hang up. Divorce was for movie stars, blues singers, jet-setters, for the class of people who exchanged partners as easily as their neighbor Manny Kaufman traded his Oldsmobile every fall for a new model. Divorce was for that woman down the street, Mrs. Gordon, whose daughter Susie had played with Ceely. The ex-Mrs. Gordon worked nights singing torch songs at the Palmer House. She dyed her hair blond, freshened her lipstick in public.

In time, the ad became so yellowed Esther feared it would crumble at the slightest touch, like the wings of a dead butterfly or moth. Meanwhile, the apartment bloomed in her imagination. She envisioned walls the color of vanilla custard, rooms that smelled of lemon and roses. There would be just enough space for a narrow bed, her books, a radio, the dressmaker's dummy upon which she'd fitted so many of Ceely's garments. Only the plush voice of her favorite radio host and the ticking of the clock above the stove would breach the silence. Occasionally, when the el rumbled by, strangers would try and peer through her windows and wonder about the life inside.

The first time Esther showed up without Marty, Jack looked confused. She sat across from him, on the edge of the wooden chair, snapping and unsnapping the clasp on her purse, which rested stiffly in her lap. She kept her coat buttoned up. "My husband must never find out that I'm here," she said.

Jack had little to offer, yet Esther found him oddly reassuring, like the rosary Ella Tucker, in 3A, fingered all day. Ella had those beads to soothe her spirits; Esther had Jack, with the messy desk and the clanging radiator.

Jack reported that Ceely was working in a hardware store. "Dunnaway's."

"Well, that's good. At least it's not your everyday Ace," Esther replied. "Dunnaway's," she said, trying it on for size.

In the silence that followed, her eyes settled on Jack's desk, on the litter of paper, Styrofoam cups, stale Chinese carryout, empty Coke cans. How could she trust anything that emerged from that mess? Yet she did. Perhaps it was Jack's voice that kept her coming back for more. It was as calm and reassuring as his handshake. The first time they'd met she hadn't wanted to let go. Or perhaps it was the easy way he rolled those metal balls.

"Qigong," he explained, when Esther finally got up the nerve to ask. "They're Chinese. The object is to roll them without letting them touch. They clear the mind, circulate life energy. They're even good for my arthritis." Jack shrugged, as if even he didn't quite believe all that he was saying.

"So you've been to China?" Esther realized how little she knew of Jack.

"Nah. They sell these in Chinatown. Between the paper fans and the mah-jongg sets." He reached across the desk. "Here," he said, his arm outstretched, the metal balls nesting firmly in his cupped hand. "Give me your hand."

Stubbornly, Esther tightened her grip on the purse and thought of Ceely, four years old, refusing to hold her hand as they crossed the street.

"Come on, Esther. Hold out your hand."

Jack's hand was steady. His nails were clipped and, given the condition of his desk, surprisingly clean. A gold band flashed on his left ring finger. "Come on," he coaxed, grinning at her. "Don't be afraid."

"I'm not afraid," she muttered, her gaze fixed on the glinting ring. She looked away. He's a detective, after all. Could he sense her fear that one touch and she might never let go?

Nervously, she extended a cupped hand, managing to hold it steady as he slipped the balls into her palm. They were warm. Jack's warmth. She rocked them gently in the palm of her hand, as if she were handling robin's eggs. Ceely once carried an egg around in a box lined with cotton balls and satin scraps from Esther's fabric pile. She'd enrolled in an after-school babysitting class, and for one week was expected to look after that egg, guard it with her life. Midweek, Ceely abandoned the project. "It's boring," she said, when Esther urged her to stick with it. Ceely slouched and grimaced and called it stupid. "I don't want to babysit!" Then she stormed outside, smashed the egg on the sidewalk, and sashayed back into the house as if she might earn a merit badge for insubordination.

Esther's cupped hand started to shake and then the balls crashed to the floor and rolled under the radiator. "Look what I've done!" she cried. "I broke them."

Jack, on hands and knees, grinned up at Esther as he fished them out, and assured her they didn't break. "It's harder than it looks," he said, flopping back into his chair. "But you'll get the hang of it."

After that, Esther trusted everything Jack told her. At one visit, when she asked if Ceely might have been brainwashed by one of those groups that takes all your money, he threw back his head and laughed. "No, Ceely isn't party to anything like that."

Ceely changed jobs often. After the hardware store, she worked in quick succession at the A&P, a bookstore, and a coffee shop in Burlington that sold her mugs.

"Odd jobs," Jack said.

"So she wasn't fired?"

"Not as far as I can tell."

"That's your job, isn't it?"

"What?"

"To be able to tell."

He shrugged. "I suppose it is." Then he rummaged through a drawer, pulled out what appeared to be a mug, handed it to Esther, and told her to turn it over. The letters CL had been scratched into the rough bottom. Esther traced the surface with her finger, as if she were caressing her daughter's auburn hair. The mug, cold and awkward, reminded Esther of the Mother's Day gifts Ceely had brought home over the years—crocheted pot holders, picture frames made from popsicle sticks, spindly plants in Dixie cups.

Esther drank her afternoon tea from the mug, always returning it, before Marty got home, to the mahogany breakfront where she stored the Passover dishes and china teacups. She drank her tea and wrote letters to Ceely, every one of which came back unopened. *We had our first crisp fall day today. I had to put on a coat when I ran my errands. I needed things for our new place. This and that. Nothing special. Our new apartment is* much smaller than the house, but don't worry, there's plenty of room for you.

Sometimes Esther reported what she'd read in the newspaper. She knew that Ceely received the same news in Vermont, just as she knew that she and Mrs. Singh read the same *Sun-Times* every morning, though that didn't stop the two of them from clucking over one story or another as they passed on the stairway.

Esther bought cards for Ceely on all the holidays. Rosh Hashanah. Chanukah. She found a Thanksgiving card that unfurled into a crown of turkey tail feathers. Sometimes she included a swatch of fabric from a garment that she was sewing. She even offered to make something for Ceely. I found some fleece the other day. It comes in jewel tones. I imagine you can use warm clothes in Vermont.

Esther slipped a twenty-dollar bill into a birthday card. Buy yourself something special. A box of chocolates, perhaps.

She thought of Marty, who never brought her chocolates. "You're always on a diet," he would say. But that wasn't the point. Flowers, Marty. You could bring me flowers, if you're so concerned about my weight. To Ceely, she wrote, Or if you prefer, treat yourself to flowers.

She never wrote about Marty, not even when he started taking pills for high blood pressure, because it was Marty, she was sure, who had driven Ceely away. Esther never breathed a word of her theory to Marty, not even the morning he stormed out over the mismatched argyle socks. Where did blame get you? Look at the Tuckers in 3A. After their daughter died of that rare bone cancer, Ella told anyone within listening range that her husband Manny's cousin had died of the same disease, at the exact same age. The mailman, the checker at the Jewel, the young girl who worked at the dry cleaners, all heard about Manny's defective gene pool. Then one day, Manny didn't come home.

Esther and Ella used to go down for the mail at the same time every day. How many times, standing there in the foyer, had she lent a friendly ear after Manny took off? And when Ella cried about her dead daughter, Esther clutched the woman's hand or patted her fleshy back. Then one day, trying to console Ella, she said, "You know, there's more than one way to lose a child." Ella turned and spit on Esther's slippered feet before stalking up the stairs. After that, Esther started to listen for Ella; she waited until she heard Ella's door click shut a second time before tiptoeing downstairs for her mail.

Esther set the mug on Jack's desk, held his gaze, and thanked him. Smiling regretfully, as if she already knew this was to be their last encounter, she said, "You've done all you can. But you can't bring Ceely back."

"My door's always open," Jack said. He set the metal balls on his desk and escorted Esther to the door. He started to open it, but when he hesitated, Esther recalled that once she'd gotten close enough to smell licorice on his breath. One more step and they'd be that close again. Nervously, she reached for the handle, but he stopped her and she felt her heart race, the color rise to her face. Was this the reason she'd kept returning to Jack? Had she been waiting for a moment like this?

She was imagining the licorice she might taste on his lips when Jack interrupted. In his soothing, familiar voice—it sounded like woodwinds—he said, "Listen, Esther, people leave for all kinds of reasons. Reasons that make sense to them." He paused. "But not to anybody else. Do you understand what I'm saying?"

She nodded, then proudly tilted her chin. But she did not understand. Ceely had gone away to that small college in Vermont, dropped out after the first year, and didn't come home. Where was the reason in that?

One day, over lunch at Wing Yee's, Lorraine says to Esther, "Where are we going to put all the bodies?"

"All I know is, cremation isn't right," says Esther, who intends to be buried in the ground, wearing her blue silk dress with the dyed-to-match shoes. She is leaving nothing to chance. From time to time, she reminds Ceely and Sophie (there's no point involving Barry) about the folder labeled, My Funeral. "It's all there, in black and white. In a drawer in the breakfront, just below the china teacups."

Esther's mourners are to be ushered in to the strains of Pachelbel's Canon and file out to "Stranger in Paradise," the Tony Bennett version. The postburial menu is to include cheese blintzes, minibagels with lox, and bite-sized rugelach from the German bakery on Montrose. Lorraine has agreed to prepare a chopped-liver swan and promised to use pimento olives for the eyes, as Toots Lustig had done. Should she predecease Esther, Sophie will step in, but without all the fanfare. Sophie is also in charge of the flowers. Bougainvillea. Esther has threatened to haunt her granddaughter should a single carnation be on display.

After the waitress sets down a pot of tea, Esther reminds Lorraine about the chopped-liver swan. "And don't forget the parsley tail feathers, or my mother-in-law will have a fit."

"Your mother-in-law is dead," Lorraine says, giving Esther a baleful look. "And besides, we were talking about cremation."

Impatiently, Esther says, "You know I already have my plot."

What Lorraine doesn't know is that Esther and Marty fought over the plots. At some point during their row, Esther recklessly suggested cremation, which was practically unheard of back then. They'd been heading to the cemetery to check out the plots, which some loudmouth from the temple brotherhood had been pushing. "Maybe we should consider cremation," Esther said. The idea popped into her mind unbidden. The mere concept was exotic, foreign, remote as India. Cremation had nothing to do with their life.

"Cremation?" Marty slapped the steering wheel; his face turned red. He accused Esther of wanting to use their burial money for a new refrigerator.

She denied it, but agreed that he had a point. "All that money, Marty. For what?"

"So I'm right!" he crowed.

When she stood her ground, he argued that he didn't want to be burned.

"You won't know the difference," she said, not certain she was correct. All she knew of cremation came from pictures in *Life*. Giant funeral pyres. Bodies strewn with flower petals, before the flames consumed them.

"So now you're an authority on the afterlife?" Marty was shouting.

"Then you buy a plot, and I'll be cremated," she snapped. Briefly, she felt cheered by the thought. The possibility of spending eternity away from Marty, no more quarrels followed by difficult silences, buoyed her spirits. But then she turned and caught a glimpse of his profile, his round, ruddy cheeks, the irregular bump at the bridge of his nose, which she sometimes caressed. She observed the way his hands gripped the steering wheel, at ten o'clock and two, the same way he'd taught her to drive. There he sat, hunched over the wheel, heeding the traffic, guarding against oncoming cars, defending them against impending disaster. She leaned back in her seat and sighed, content to let him steer them safely to their destination.

They drove the rest of the way in silence, and most of the way home, until Marty said, "Come on, Esther. I'll take you out to dinner."

"Are you crazy? We just spent all that money on plots."

She asked him to stop at the Jewel, where she ran in for milk and cheddar cheese and English muffins. She got a rain check for the butter that was on sale. She smiled at the thought of telling Marty that on a day when she'd been planning her death, she asked for a rain check. But when she got to the car, he was pounding the steering wheel, demanding to know what took her so long.

Now she's grateful for the plot, which is what she tells Lorraine. "It gives me peace of mind, knowing exactly where I'll be." Then she points out that Lorraine still hasn't dealt with her mother, still on the mantel with all the stuff that gets left there during the course of a day: coffee mugs, books, old newspapers, yesterday's mail. Lorraine's mother has been there for as long as Esther can remember, packed in the kind of decorative tin that might otherwise contain English toffee or fancy tea.

Esther has no intention of hanging around collecting dust like that while Ceely and Barry dither over how to dispose of her remains. Or worse, they'll forget she's there, or lose her. "Have you seen Ma?" Ceely will say, to which Barry will reply, "Ma?" Charges and countercharges will fly, accusations and recriminations will be set loose, and Esther won't even be able to intervene, as she's been doing all her life. Quiet! Both of you. I've had enough. The thought that her own children won't find the time to properly dispose of her remains fills her with sadness.

When Marty died, Esther was in such a state that everything

was over before she knew it. Only after he was in the ground did she learn that he'd been buried in his brown tweed jacket and a pair of ordinary slacks, the ones he wore when they went to the movies or to the Pearlmans' for an evening of bridge. At least Ceely and Barry, who'd made all the arrangements, remembered his tallis.

A light snow had started to fall as they buried Marty. Several inches had accumulated by the time they reached Ceely and Lenny's home. It snowed all afternoon, but the people who crowded into the house to pay their respects were too busy filling their plates to notice. Esther filled a plate, too. Then she put on her coat and boots, and with Marty's astrakhan hat and gloves in one hand, the plate in the other, she headed outdoors. But before she reached the foot of the driveway, Ceely was calling to her and then Lenny was at her side leading her back inside. She tried to resist, but he was persistent and strong. When she tried to explain that Marty needed something to eat, and she'd never sleep, not as long as she thought of her husband in the ground without his hat and gloves, Lenny tightened his hold on her. "His hands used to get so cold," Esther cried.

Now she's arguing with Lorraine in favor of a proper burial, though perhaps her friend has a point. Had Marty yielded to Esther's wild suggestion, he wouldn't have needed his hat and gloves on that cold winter day.

Esther has always struggled with an extra five or ten pounds, which she has managed to lose for special occasions, such as an impending wedding or bar mitzvah. Once, she lost an entire dress size before a Caribbean cruise. The term yo-yo dieting might have been invented for Esther, who has been on every diet from Atkins to South Beach to a particularly malodorous regimen in which she ate nothing but cabbage soup for eleven days.

Now, casting a critical eye upon her reflection in the bedroom mirror, she is pleased to see that the blue dress still fits. There's even room to spare at the waist and hips, though the hemline falls farther below her knees than it did years ago. Esther is shrinking and there isn't a diet in the world to remedy that.

She grabs hold of some fabric and hikes the dress up. "Much better," she says, nodding at her image.

This she won't say aloud, not even to Lorraine, who knows her plans, that she shudders at the thought of a stranger, probably a man, possibly someone who can barely read, straining to squeeze her lifeless body into the dress, the way she once struggled to put silver lamé capri pants on Ceely's Barbie doll. To avoid such indignity, Esther tries the dress on twice a year to be sure that, when the time comes, it slips on like a glove.

If Marty were here, she'd ask his opinion. But then, tilting her head to one side, studying her image, she recalls how Marty clammed up when she asked his advice. When she pressed, he'd reply, "If I tell you it looks good, you won't believe me." She'd glare at him and say, "You have an opinion on everything, until I ask for one," to which he'd say, "Just tell me what you want me to say. Should I tell you it's too long? Too short? You tell me, Esther." That's how it went with the two of them. Still, if he were here, she would say, "What do you think?" It's so lonely arguing with herself.

Again, she raises the hem. The shorter length is so pleasing that she considers taking the dress to Alberta, whose flawless French seams and painstaking stitches rivaled those of the city's top plastic surgeons. Then, remembering that Alberta is gone, she lets the fabric fall. Alberta, in her knitted slippers, her stockings rolled below her knees, seated at the sewing machine in the back of Ziegler's Cleaners, or settled in her tufted easy chair, hands flying over fabric like a pair of doves released from silk scarves, had been as reassuring to Esther as the cat curled up between the geranium pots, sunning itself in the store's front window. Alberta, old Mr. Ziegler, the cat, had been part of the fabric of Esther's life. Then one day, Alberta was gone, and the kid who started filling in more and more for old Mr. Ziegler couldn't say why. In time, Mr. Ziegler told Esther, "Alberta's got that macular degeneration."

Once more, Esther hikes the dress up and agrees with herself that the shorter length is more becoming. If her hands weren't so warped, so bent out of shape, she could stitch a hem, the way Mrs. Rothstein, the seamstress in her father's shop, had instructed her all those years ago. Perhaps Mrs. Singh wouldn't mind. After all, she and her husband used to run that dress shop on Devon. Yes, she'll ask her neighbor. But then she'd have to explain her plans. Once more, she lets the hem drop, sighs, and thinks that next time she wears the dress, she'll be laid out in a pine box. "Nobody will know the difference," she tells her reflection.

She bought the dress during one of her svelte phases to wear on the high holidays. This was the time of year when the women of Congregation Emanuel behaved more like Hollywood starlets on Oscar night than penitents appealing for another year of life to a judgmental and potentially wrathful God. The rest of the year the sanctuary was as empty as a Broadway theater during a blizzard. On the high holidays it was standing room only.

The sanctuary was cavernous and severe. Leaded windows depicting the Exodus from Egypt, blocked the light. A gilded Star of David emblazoned on the ceiling loomed over the congregation like the omniscient eye of God. Yet on the holiest days of the year, a time for reflection and reverence and awe, a carnival atmosphere prevailed. The sanctuary became charged with the rustle of silk, the intoxicating mélange of perfume, the glitter of gemstones and gold. Charm bracelets jingled like wind chimes when the pages of prayer books were turned.

Esther, who'd disdained the yearly fashion parade, who scorned the women for tossing mink stoles over empty seats to save them for tardy friends, who loathed the hypocrisy of "once a year" Jews, got swept up in the fervor that svelte year. It was as if she were possessed by the thinner woman who'd taken over her soft, round body. Zaftig, Marty called her. He preferred her that way.

It was during that svelte year that Hank Stammler started sniffing around. Esther fell so hard for her neighbor's attention that she could hardly eat. And when she was as thin as she'd ever be, she bypassed her father's dress shop for Saks Fifth Avenue and paid full price for an Italian silk knit dress—a simple, blue sleeveless sheath with a matching bolero jacket. She loved the shimmering satin lining and the rhinestone button, fat as a golf ball, that fastened at the neck.

The Stammlers and Lustigs had always been cordial neighbors, sharing cups of sugar and accepting each other's packages from the mailman. Suddenly, Hank was hanging around, engaging Esther in long conversations. He'd cross over into their yard, stand there in his Bermuda shorts and huaraches, jingling the change in his pockets and shooting the breeze, while Esther, who had only ever plunked a few six-packs of petunias and sweet alyssum into a patch of dirt outside the back door, planted delphinium and salvia, cleome and stock. That summer, she put in rose bushes, upon which, Marty said, she lavished more care than she'd ever shown to her own two children. She started gardening in halter-tops and wore sunglasses that made her feel like Jackie Kennedy. On the days Hank didn't show up, she was cross with the children; on the days when he did, she acceded to Ceely and Barry's every demand, while fantasizing a life with the man next door—the sex, the scintillating conversations, the laughter. They'd be soul mates, a concept Marty failed to understand. "Are we soul mates, Marty?" she'd once asked. Without looking up from the crossword, he said, "Why not? Whatever you say, Essie."

Well, she could hardly blame him for that listless response. She'd only just run across the idea while reading a magazine under the hair dryer at the beauty parlor. Still. Together, they could have pondered its meaning and perhaps discovered some way in which it applied to them. Or she might laugh. "Soul mates! That's the most ridiculous thing I've ever heard." And Marty might say, "Perhaps, but we are something Esther. We'll just have to figure out what it is."

The next week, she asked Marty, "Am I fun to be with?" The question was part of a relationship IQ test she'd found in a magazine in the dentist's waiting room. Marty caught her off guard when he said, "Actually, Esther, I've been thinking that lately you've lost some of your zip." Being a pharmacist, he was in the habit of recommending tonics for people, so she tried not to take it too hard.

But then she thought of her friend, Ruthie Sherman, who, one week after her fortieth birthday, left a tuna noodle casserole and a note for her husband while he was playing tennis at his club. Ruthie hopped in her car and drove to Santa Fe, where she rented a casita, took painting classes, and grew her hair long. She returned one year later with her hair swept up in a silver barrette and a carload of paintings—lurid pictures of desert sunsets. Once Esther got as far as preparing a tuna casserole for Marty. But by the time dinner rolled around she was seated across the table from him, and all during the meal she tried to imagine him eating alone. She wondered if he would bother to chew with his mouth shut? Would he reach for second helpings, or would he be so distraught by her absence that he'd pick at his food until it turned cold? The image of Marty picking at his food kept her grounded.

But that svelte summer she thought often of Ruthie's casserole. Hank would stroll over, like the time she was digging around the rose bushes, and stand there, hands deep in the pockets of his Bermuda shorts, describing the plot of an Italian movie he'd just seen or a new restaurant that served great burritos. On one such occasion, Esther grabbed a worm that was burrowing back into the ground and dangled it in the air. She smiled up at Hank, who had already shared with her his love of fishing, and in a smoky voice said, "Here, a present for you."

Hank, who charmed Esther with little Spanish phrases he'd picked up on a one-week, all expenses paid trip to Acapulco, said she was *muy* funny. "*Muy, mucho* funny, Esther." Frightened that the flirtation was getting out of hand, she said that she really wasn't all that funny and that she had to get Barry to his guitar lesson.

In the car, with her son slouched in the seat beside her, his baseball cap covering his eyes, she imagined driving to Lake Geneva with Hank. She'd already bought a copy of *Rod and Reel,* so they'd have plenty to discuss. (When Marty cast a quizzical eye at the magazine, she lied and said the mailman delivered it to the wrong house.) Hank's van would be loaded with fishing rods and tackle boxes and a coffee can full of worms from Esther's garden.

By the time Esther dropped Barry off for his lesson, her fantasy had bloomed like her prize American Beauty roses. She was asking Hank to bait her hooks, and he was saying, *No problema, Esther.* And when something caught on the line, he reeled it in for her and pulled the hook out of its puckering mouth. Hank was at her service. Rub my feet, Hank. Fetch me that book, will you? Be a love, Hank, and scratch my back. Oooh. That's good. A little higher. No, higher. Lower. Stop! There. Ahh. No matter what she said, his response was always the same. *No problema, Esther.*

At dinner that evening, Esther looked across the table and saw Hank's face superimposed on her husband's. In bed, after Marty pecked her on the cheek and said good night, she imagined sex in Hank's van, arms and legs flailing among the fishing gear. She could smell the leather seats and the loamy dirt in the coffee can full of worms. At breakfast the next morning, the littlest things annoyed her. The way Marty creased the newspaper after folding it in thirds. The way he shook his vitamin from the bottle. She wanted her thoughts to go away. She wanted to be nothing more than Esther Lustig, wife of Martin, mother of Barry and Ceely. She wanted her obsession to run its course, like a bout of the flu or a mysterious virus. But she also wanted it to go on forever.

Then one day, Sylvia Stammler let herself into Esther's kitchen and between sobs managed to convey that Hank had run out for a pack of cigarettes the previous night and never returned. Sometime after midnight he called to say she shouldn't wait up for him. When Sylvia snapped her fingers and said, "He left. Just like that," Esther came to, as if Sylvia were a hypnotist releasing her from a spell. That could have been me. Saddled with a no-goodnik who takes off. Just like that. Suddenly, she saw Hank cringe and step back that time she dangled the worm. And she saw Marty, relaxing in the evening after a hard day at work, pencil poised over the crossword, brow furrowed, waiting patiently for the right word. And then she started to cry. Sylvia must have assumed the tears were for her, but every last drop was for Esther, grateful to be released to her familiar, comfortable zaftig body.

On Sundays, Lenny picks up Esther on his way home from the lab. As they drive to Wing Yee's, she scolds him for working weekends and he patiently explains that nematodes haven't yet grasped the notion of a day of rest. At Wing Yee's, Lenny leaves the motor running so Esther can listen to the radio while he runs in to pick up their order. Then he drives home, kamikaze style, racing through yellow lights, lurching through stop signs, until Esther feels nearly overcome by the sudden stops and starts and the pervading smell of Chinese food.

Their arrival precipitates near-hysteria as everyone rushes to get the food to the table before it turns cold. Coats get flung over chairs, bodies collide in the rush from kitchen to dining room. Everyone talks at once. "We need another spoon." "Did you remember the fortune cookies?" "Josh, turn off that computer!" "Where's the soy sauce?" "Ma, do you want chopsticks?" though Esther hasn't been able to manage chopsticks for years. Then comes the frantic inspection of cartons, the sorting out of kung pao chicken from Buddha's delight, and sometimes the assignment of blame for a missing order. At last, they are seated and cartons are passed, along with comparisons of this week's order to last. Saltier. Blander. Too many bean sprouts and not enough shrimp. Too hot. "As in *picante*," Lenny might say.

Then the meal is over. Ceely, Sophie, and Josh clear their plates, abandoning Lenny and Esther, who knows that the minute she gets up somebody will drive her home. Sometimes it feels as if all the rushing had been set in place to hurry the evening along to the moment when someone reaches for the car keys and hustles her out the door. Another Sunday meal completed, a race to the finish from the moment Ceely phoned in the order and asked, "How soon will it be ready?"

But for a while, it is just Esther and Lenny.

This evening, Lenny is telling Esther that if his latest grant application is rejected, he'll have to fire two research assistants. Esther issues some consoling remarks, glad that for once she has something to offer. Rejection, she understands. But beyond that, Lenny might as well be speaking Milo's language, one that employs the Cyrillic alphabet. Hard as she tries, she can't quite grasp her son-in-law's work, which entails the search for extending life. Turn off the aging switch. That's what Lenny wants to do. When he tells her his grant application proposes to build on earlier successes with yeast and a particular kind of worm, Esther considers telling him about the pack of expired Red Star yeast in her refrigerator. But then Lenny, who has been waving his chopsticks for emphasis, bursts forth, "The question is, why can't we do the same with people?" With a gesture of finality, he plunks down his chopsticks on the clean white cloth.

At times like this Esther finds herself scrutinizing Lenny's face, as if after all these years, something new might present itself. He has a strong nose and a fringe of graying hair, the texture of Brillo. In his frenzied, professorial state, he reminds her of the fuzzy *New Yorker* cartoon characters she so enjoys. The first time Ceely brought Lenny home, Esther could barely contain her disappointment. She'd been expecting someone with a bit more dash, a more even temper, the kind of person you could count on when your car conked out or the toilet wouldn't stop running. Yet for all his brilliance, Lenny Frankel was the last person you'd call on in a pinch. She's long suspected that his incompetence was willful, a deliberate strategy to insulate himself from the everyday tasks of life. Yet her son-in-law has grown on her. And when he talks about his work, his features, normally inscrutable, rearrange themselves into something open and appealing.

Now, trying to sound like one of those clever radio hosts, Terry Gross, or that smarty-pants, Ira Flatow, someone with the ability to appear informed while knowing nothing really about the matter at hand, she says, "You mean to tell me that if I were a worm, you could do something to make me live longer?"

Lenny removes his glasses and rubs his eyes. Their color— one blue, one brown—have the power to disconcert her. They are like Lenny, Esther thinks, one part brilliant scientist, the other, *haimish* son-in-law. The problem is, she never knows which Lenny she is talking to. "If you were a worm?" he says. He blows on the lenses, then polishes them with a napkin, slowly picking his words, as if the deliberate spacing of each utterance will make everything clear. That is something else she likes about Lenny. Even her simplest questions earn his utmost consideration.

He puts his glasses back and gazes at her from behind thick lenses. "Not a worm, Esther." He pauses. "C. elegans." He draws the word out, pronouncing it as if he were ordering something off a French menu. "The little nematode. It's brilliant, really." Then he plunges his chopsticks into a cold carton of sesame noodles, which earlier had been the subject of considerable debate over whether Mr. Yee had skimped on the peanuts.

All this talk of worms, Esther thinks. But Lenny wouldn't appreciate the irony, wouldn't stop to consider that one might not want to hear about worms while eating noodles. Nor would it occur to him that despite all his journal articles, the chapters in textbooks, the invitations to lecture in faraway places, despite the hobnobbing with other experts, and the endowed chair (he is the Morris and Sylvia Fischbach Professor of Molecular Biology) that Esther once famously asked to sit on, despite all that, she can tell Lenny Frankel a thing or two about getting old. And not once will she have to talk about worms at the dinner table.

"Brilliant. Yes," she agrees, her voice trailing off. She fingers her chopsticks, still encased in their paper wrapper, and considers the infinite frustrations of living in an aging body.

She might remind Lenny that once she'd wielded these sticks with the same precision as he. In fact, it was she who introduced the family to chopsticks the year she took Mrs. Chen's cooking class in Old Town, bought a wok and five-spice powder. She wonders whether older Chinese share her problem: at a certain age, hobbled by arthritis, do they switch to forks? Or perhaps no accommodations are made for this particular infirmity and eventually they starve to death. Perhaps this was how the Chinese dispensed with their elders, the way Eskimos are said to set their aging parents adrift on ice floes. She is just about to say, "What's the point of living longer, when daily our bodies defeat us?" when Ceely appears, already buttoning her coat. "Lenny?" The uptick she delivers at the end of his name sounds like a prearranged signal, which Lenny misses. Frowning, Ceely repeats his name. Then, with deliberation, says, "It's too late for lectures. My mother is tired."

"Leave him alone," Esther scolds. "He's explaining something." Smiling, she turns to her son-in-law.

Lenny hunches his shoulders and rises as he begins to stack the dishes.

Esther reaches over, sets a hand on his to stop him. "I'll help with that," she says.

"No!" Ceely snaps. She fishes the car keys from her purse. "Lenny can do them." Then, atoning for her outburst, she says, "Besides, you must be exhausted."

"Not really." Esther sits up straight, sets her hands in her lap, and smiles, an obsequious child hoping to stay up past her bedtime.

"Well, I'm tired," Ceely sighs, jingling the keys, as if Esther were a baby in need of pacifying. "Even if you're not."

Esther consults her watch, Marty's old Timex with the expandable band and the big numbers. It's early. She looks at Ceely, her golden child who morphed into an angry teen and then an officious adult. The adolescent rage is gone, but so are the soft contours. If Ceely were a chair, she'd be hard, unyielding. Utilitarian. "Perhaps you should see a doctor," Esther says.

"A doctor?"

"If you're so exhausted." Esther folds her napkin and places it to the left of where her plate had been. At least Ceely doesn't use paper. She sets out her good dishes, cloth napkins. "It's not even eight o'clock," Esther says, as she presses the napkin with the flat of her hand. "Besides. How can you be tired when you didn't cook?"

"What did you say?" Ceely's nostrils flare; her face flushes. She flings her purse over her shoulder, and turns to exit.

Esther looks at Lenny, beseeching him for support, but his head is bowed as he busies himself with the dishes. Then she turns to Ceely. "Stop," she says. "I merely said that you shouldn't be tired, given that you didn't cook dinner." She smiles ruefully. "Remember the old joke?"

"Joke?" Ceely's face falls, resistance yielding to resignation.

Esther, stifling the urge to tell her daughter to put on some lipstick, says, "You know. The one about the reservations?" She turns to Lenny. "I'm sure you've heard it."

Lenny glances at Ceely, who shoots him a warning look.

"I'm sure Lenny's heard it," Esther insists.

"Heard what?" Ceely sinks into a chair, letting her purse drop to the floor.

"The joke about the reservations."

"Tell me," she sighs.

"Never mind. I'm sure you've heard it. It's old as the hills."

Ceely jackknifes out of her chair, grabs her purse, and rattles the keys. "Will you please just tell the fucking joke, so we can get out of here?"

"Ceely!" The dishes in Lenny's hands crash to the table. He glares at his wife. "That's enough." Turning to Esther, who is folding and unfolding her napkin, he says, "We'll clear up, Esther. Then I'll drive you home."

Esther, fighting back tears, nods, then turns to Ceely. "Reservations," she whispers. "It's what a Jewish woman makes for dinner."

To Lenny she says, "You have work to do. Ceely will take me."

Esther tossed and turned that night. She wanted to blame her restlessness on Mr. Yee's free hand with the MSG. Or perhaps she should have rejected that second cup of tea. Whatever the reason, she lay in bed unable to erase from her mind the image of Ceely buttoning her coat, jangling the car keys, rushing her out the door.

Esther doesn't want to live with her daughter. Even worse is the thought of living with her son and that malingering wife of his, Sheila, always in bed with a bad back. Doped up, too, with Barry's help. Esther is as sure of that as she is that one day Barry Lustig, DDS, will lose his license for pushing drugs. No. She doesn't want to live with any of them.

She thinks of old Mrs. Abelson, who lived with her son and daughter-in-law and their four children, one of whom had been Ceely's best friend in grade school. Esther has long forgotten the girl's name, but she remembers the girl's mother.

She still can picture Faye Abelson on the front porch reading when Esther stopped by to collect Ceely. Faye, barely glancing up from her book, inclined her head toward the door, and said, "I think the girls are inside."

Once, Faye was reading *Light in August*. Esther, who had been reading one of those books recommended for the beach, wondered if she should go back to school like Faye, who was studying for an advanced degree in English literature. But Marty would only dismiss the idea, find some way to make her feel even smaller than she did standing on the Abelson's sagging porch wishing she had the time to sit in a wicker rocker reading Faulkner. Just as she started to berate herself for caving in to Marty's bullying put-downs, a shriek erupted from somewhere inside, followed by a barrage of Yiddish and English, and then a slamming of doors. "My mother-in-law," Faye drawled, as if enervated by the heat from that fictional Mississippi place whose name Esther never could pronounce. Faye gave the slightest nod toward the screen door, which had been aggressively clawed by the cats, and repeated that the girls were inside.

Esther was wondering whether to knock, walk right in, or ring the bell, which she suspected might be out of order, when Faye shouted, "Ma!"

In a flash, old Mrs. Abelson appeared in the doorway, wiping her hands on a print apron. "Damn dog," she hissed. "Ate the rolls."

"Did anyone remember to feed him?" Faye asked, without enthusiasm. And then, "Are the girls still inside?"

Mrs. Abelson held up a finger and said, "Wait," as if otherwise, God forbid, Faye might have to pull herself up from the chair and go in search of the girls. After the old woman scurried away, Faye slumped deeper into her rocker and sighed. "That woman is a whirling dervish. She doesn't know the meaning of the word *sit*."

Esther understood from her own mother's twice-yearly visits—at the high holidays and at Passover—that Mrs. Abelson was afraid to sit. These older women knew their place, staying tucked away, fading into the background. Mostly, they tended the kitchen, where they learned to make themselves indispensable.

Whenever Esther's mother came to visit, she'd charge around the kitchen in a pink sweat suit, rubber gloves, and pursed lips, cleaning the refrigerator, tossing out empty cereal boxes, and rearranging the pots and pans. She consolidated the dregs of

Cheerios, Rice Krispies, and Frosted Flakes into one box, which inevitably led to an uproar at breakfast when the stale mixture tumbled into the children's bowls. All her efforts backfired. By the third day, Marty was fuming and Esther was promising that her mother's next visit would be even shorter.

Esther would never interfere with Ceely's kitchen. She certainly wouldn't accept an invitation to move in. Still, it would be nice to be asked. She imagined Ceely saying: "Ma? You know that extra bedroom?" Then Esther could reply, "Thank you very much. I appreciate the offer, but I can take care of myself."

Sometimes Esther wondered whether Ceely would have turned out differently if she hadn't panicked all those years ago. But Barry was only six months old, Marty had just opened the drugstore on Touhy Avenue, and twice a week she was helping with the books. Then Helen had an idea. "What you have to do, Esther, is take a hot mustard bath. Then you ride the Bobs."

"A roller coaster? Are you crazy?"

"You asked my advice. That's my advice."

Esther remembered the way Helen gripped her hand as they approached the top. And when they plunged back toward earth Helen shrieked and laughed like she was drunk on champagne. She was eager to ride again, but Esther felt light-headed and woozy. For days, she kept running to the bathroom, checking for blood. A week had passed when she reported to Helen, "Nothing. Not even a speck."

"In that case, you're stuck," Helen said. "Stuck is stuck."

Esther never breathed a word of this to anyone, not even to Marty. Still, over the years there had been times when she'd wondered if somehow Ceely knew. There was that time when Ceely ran away, though Esther had secretly blamed Marty for their daughter's rebellion. Now, Ceely has been touting that assisted living joint, as if it were her turn to try and get rid of Esther.

Esther loved Ceely. She'd loved her from the moment the nurse placed the swaddled infant in her arms and said, "Esther, here's your baby." Esther's love never wavered, not even when Ceely disappeared to that commune in Vermont and returned all of Esther's letters unopened. If anything, Esther's love bloomed in those days, expanded to fill the void created by the pain of her daughter's rejection. Oh, how she'd loved her. But had she ever said so? How easy it would have been to whisper I love you while kissing her daughter good night, or ushering her out the door on a school morning. I love you. Yet it was possible that in all these years she'd never said so, not in so many words. But Ceely knew. She had to know. A mother loves a daughter, even if you can't say so out loud.

Isn't that what Esther had learned from her mother, who warded off the evil eye by rapping her knuckles on the table three times, or muttering "poo, poo, poo," whenever she spoke her children's names? Keep your good fortune to yourself or you'll invite disaster. Say anything good to or about your children, and the evil spirits will find them. That had been Mrs. Glass's motto. How different from today's mothers, showering their children with praise for every little effort. Even breathing! Esther is certain that nothing good can come from such unrestrained veneration.

Esther's mother, on the other hand, had been as blatant with her disapproval as she was withholding and stingy with her praise. Not that she articulated her disdain. Mrs. Glass had other ways of expressing displeasure. Pursed lips. Narrowed eyes. Silence.

Her silence could be deafening. Especially when it came to the coat. During the long stretches that she was in Florida, Mrs. Glass stored her mink with her son and daughter-in-law. Upon her return visits to Chicago, before Esther had pulled out of the airport parking lot, Mrs. Glass would say, "Tomorrow, we'll go for the coat."

The next day, Esther and her mother would drive to Harry and Clara's to pick up the coat, and for the duration of Mrs. Glass's visit, the coat moved in with Esther and Marty. Then, on the day before Mrs. Glass returned to Miami, the coat went back to Harry and Clara's.

It was on one of those drives to return the coat that Esther heard herself saying, "What does her closet have that mine doesn't?" The words, brittle and harsh, caught Esther off guard. Though a cold rain was falling, she cracked the window open, hoping to rid the air of all her hurt feelings and anger. But her words loomed in the silence, hovering like the gray November clouds that dampened the day.

Mrs. Glass, unruffled by Esther's outburst, sat erect, her gaze fixed straight ahead, as if she'd been assigned to scout the horizon for marauders and took her job to heart. The coat rested on her lap, cocooned in a garment bag left over from the days when her husband ran a dress and fur shop. Her gnarled hands, freckled with age, were planted firmly on top of the bag.

The women rode in silence, the only sound coming from the rain, which earlier in the day had been forecast as snow.

At a red light, Esther broke the silence. "I asked you a question," she said, her voice sounding eerily controlled. She glared at her mother's profile, willing her to turn and address her.

"What was the question?" Mrs. Glass asked, her eyes fixed on the road.

"You heard me," Esther snapped.

"Oy, please. What do you want from me?" Mrs. Glass shifted in her seat, then ran her hand across the garment bag, as if she were stroking a cat.

"Look at me, Ma," Esther pleaded. "I'm talking to you." But

her mother stared steadfastly ahead, stiff as the mannequins in her husband's dress and fur shop.

Esther's favorite had been the ginger-haired model, which looked like a replica of her mother. When she was very young, she loved to run up and hug it. Once, she nearly knocked it off its stand, and her father scolded her. Then he laughed and patted her behind and sent her to the back room, where Mrs. Rothstein, the seamstress, gave her scraps of fabric to play with. Esther loved the store. Then one afternoon—she must have been in the fourth grade—she came upon her father undressing the ginger-haired mannequin. He spoke in hushed tones as he unbuttoned her blouse. "Wait till you see what I've got for you," he murmured. "Something red with navy-blue piping. You're going to love it, *tsatskeleh*." Tenderly, he stroked the dummy's cheek, then ran his hand over her ginger hair. Esther, sensing that she'd stumbled upon something too dark to comprehend, fled and avoided the store for weeks.

At the next light, Esther turned to her mother, searching for the woman who'd held such erotic sway over her father. Then, like pentimento, the young, glamorous Mrs. Glass emerged through all the layers bestowed by age. Once again, she was that pretty woman with a labile mouth and the springy, ginger hair that enjoyed straying from its tortoise barrette.

"Green light, Esther," Mrs. Glass barked, breaking the spell. "You should look where you're going."

Esther stepped on the gas and, in her frustration, shouted, "Did you hear me?" She had dinner to prepare. And Barry's teacher had scheduled a meeting, something about stolen hall passes. Or was the last meeting about the passes? Barry was always in trouble. But first, Esther had to transport the coat.

She felt like tossing it out the window. She wanted to beat it with her mother's handbag, which rode on the seat between them like another passenger. Instead, she repeated the question that had already poisoned the air. "What does her closet have that mine doesn't?"

"Close the window, Esther," Mrs. Glass said. "People will hear."

"Nobody can hear," Esther shouted and rolled down the back windows, letting cold mist spray into the car. "Besides, nobody's listening. Nobody cares. Just please answer my question."

"I don't know what you're talking about." Mrs. Glass drummed her fingers on the garment bag. "What is this closet you talk about? I don't understand."

"You know perfectly well what I'm talking about!" Esther hated the desperation in her voice, but she couldn't stop. "I just want to know what's wrong with my closet?"

The light changed and the car behind Esther's honked. "Hold your horses!" she yelled. Over the shouting she thought she heard her mother say, "You can eat off her floors."

It was true. Clara's floors sparkled. Her beds were made before breakfast. Her well-appointed rooms were cool in the summer, warm in the winter. The bathroom towels were always fresh. Clara never ran out of Saran Wrap or paper napkins or rice. Clothing hung in her closets on cedar hangers, arranged by color and function, as they might have appeared in Esther's father's dress shop all those years ago. Twice a year Clara went through her closets and made a pile for Goodwill.

Clara was the daughter that Mrs. Glass would have raised. If it bothered Mrs. Glass that Clara never invited her to spend the night, never offered to pick her up at the airport, never invited her to dinner more than once per visit, she didn't let on.

As soon as Esther pulled up in front of Clara's place, her mother unfastened her seat belt and reached for her handbag. "Wait," Esther said. She was gripping the steering wheel, afraid that if she let go her hands might do something regrettable.

Staring straight ahead, she said, "I asked you a question." Again, her voice registered eerie control. "Please say something."

"Oy, Esther." Her mother leaned over and pressed a hand on her daughter's arm. "What do you want I should say?"

Esther looked down at the hand that had flown through a kitchen restoring order, baked bread, chopped onions, diapered babies. Now it was crooked and spotted with age. She averted her gaze, only to catch a glimpse of her mother's feet. They barely touched the floor. Esther reached across the seat to lay a hand on top of her mother's, but Mrs. Glass turned and pressed her nose against the window, as if yearning for whatever lay beyond. "What do you want from me?" she whispered.

Tell me you love me, Esther wanted to say. At least let the coat hang in my closet. Tell me my closets are good enough.

Esther's mother never relented. For as long as Mrs. Glass made the trip from Miami to Chicago, her visits began with the same instruction. "Tomorrow, we'll go for the coat."

"I bet you enjoy dancing."

Esther looks up from her magazine and follows the voice across the room to where Dr. Levenson's receptionist is stationed. "Were you talking to me?"

The receptionist scans the empty waiting room to suggest the answer is obvious. "I asked if you dance."

"'Fraid not. I lost my dancing partner not so long ago." Esther shrugs and holds out her hands, as if they might at one time have held the lost partner.

"Oh." The receptionist frowns.

"Besides, I'm not so steady on my feet anymore," Esther confesses. Then she looks down, hoping to be proven wrong, hoping that her feet might spontaneously burst into a fandango. But there they sit, two swollen lumps of unmolded clay, cosseted in old brown leather pumps. It's hard to believe that they ever had danced, that they'd ever tripped lightly after Marty onto a dance floor. Cha-cha. Rumba. Waltz. They'd done it all.

Esther extends her legs and lifts her feet a few inches off the floor, as if the receptionist might want to see for herself. "My feet are swollen," she says.

"That's too bad," the receptionist replies. She begins filing her nails and Esther returns to her magazine. After reading and re-reading the same paragraph, she realizes that she has been tapping her feet—one, two, cha cha cha. She smiles. Her old feet remember. But when she glances down, she sees the same homely wallflowers, and unless her eyes are playing tricks on her, the flesh is beginning to spill over the edges. Why hadn't she worn a softer shoe? And why hadn't the receptionist, still fussing with her nails, kept her questions to herself? Do you dance? Look at her, with that tiny gemstone winking off the side of her nose. And those hands! So smooth and competent, wielding an emery board with such ease. Do you dance? She wouldn't even know the dances that Esther's feet had burned up the rug with. Burned up the rug. She wouldn't know that, either. Suddenly, Esther feels as if she is seated on the other side of an impossible divide. She's drowning. How would she describe this feeling to Lorraine? How would she measure the space that engulfs her? What would she say? If you took all the people in the world and laid them end to end . . . yes, something like that, something so implausible, yet vivid enough to convey the enormity of it all, the feeling that she could never make it to the other side where the receptionist sits shaping her pearly nails into perfect ovals. Esther glares at the young woman. If she hadn't been so nosy, Esther could be finishing that article about some town in Oklahoma that was rebuilding after a tornado. Instead, she is sitting here obsessing about the condition of her swollen feet.

The phone rings. Esther pretends to read while the receptionist confirms an appointment and issues directions to the doctor's office. She repeats the directions so many times that Esther feels like grabbing the phone and telling the caller to take a cab. But the receptionist appears animated by her task, eager to help. She has a pretty face, not unlike Esther's grandson's girlfriend, the one with the heart-shaped face and the messy hair. The receptionist's hair is held back with a pink barrette. It brings to mind all those new shampoos infused with the essence of herbs. Esther imagines it smells of rosemary or lavender or chamomile tea.

When the receptionist hangs up, Esther says, "I know some-one who sees flowering trees with pink blossoms. Even in winter."

The receptionist stares across the gulf at Esther, an eyebrow raised to convey interest.

"Clara, my sister-in-law, thought she was going crazy, but it turns out it's her macular degeneration acting up. I'm sure Dr. Levenson knows all about it. 'Phantom vision,' they call it." Esther is enjoying the sound of her own voice. It is the voice of a woman who might not have tired feet, a woman who might still have a dancing partner, a woman who commands respect. "It's not as uncommon as you'd think," she continues. "Clara's doctor told her that people see all kinds of things. Little monkeys with red hats. Teddy bears. Windmills. Sometimes Clara sees flowers in the bathroom sink. She says they're always pleasant images. But she won't tell anyone except me. She hasn't even told Harry, her husband. She's afraid people will think she's crazy."

The receptionist starts to speak, then the phone rings. Esther, grateful for the interruption, sinks back in her chair and reflects on their exchange, pleased that she spoke with such authority. The air no longer rings with her pitiful confession of bloated feet.

The door opens and an elderly couple enters. They make a beeline, as if they'd been here before, to a pair of chairs arranged on either side of an end table. Esther tries guessing which one of them is here to see Dr. Levenson.

The man helps the woman with her coat and hangs it on a hook near the door. Esther's coat—single-breasted black wool with a shawl collar—lies in a careless heap on the chair beside her. Once, it had been quite stylish. Quickly, she turns it over to hide the fact that it is missing a button, which she's been mean-ing to sew back on. She looks to see if she's been observed, but the man is handing a magazine to his wife. "You'll like this," he says.

She is trying to remember if Marty had ever been so solic-
itous—he certainly wouldn't have hung up her coat—when the
receptionist pipes up. "Well, I'm sure if you tried, you'd enjoy it."

For a second, Esther thinks the receptionist is urging the
woman to accept her husband's offering of the magazine, but
then she hears her name. "Mrs. Lustig?"

"Yes?"

"I said, 'I'm sure you'd enjoy it.'"

"Seeing things?"

"No." The receptionist smiles, as if Esther were a child who'd
just mixed up the letters of the alphabet. "Dancing," she says, with
an infantilizing emphasis on the first syllable. Then brightening,
she adds, "It will probably help with your balance, too."

Before Esther can suggest that they put their conversation
on hold now that they are no longer alone, the receptionist tells
Esther about an aunt who lives in Florida and loves to dance.
"She's kind of like those gals on that TV show. The four of them
share a house? You know the one."

*Golden Girls,* Esther says, glancing nervously at the couple.
But they appear unperturbed by the conversation. The woman is
engrossed in her magazine, scanning it with a magnifying glass,
reminding Esther of Ceely when she was learning to read, the
way she sounded out each word so that by the time she'd strung
together six or seven words it was a wonder she could make any
sense of the whole. So it's her. She's the one with the appointment, Esther is thinking, as the receptionist exclaims, "That's the
one! *Golden Girls.* Ever watch it?"

When the show premiered, Esther had been sure that one day
she'd move to California and share a place with her sister. Until
the day Anna died, she pictured the two of them, old widows, sitting on a bench overlooking the ocean. She and her sister would
spend hours on that bench, reading newspapers, tossing bread

crumbs to pigeons, taking in the sun. They'd share tidbits from the news, like the man across the waiting room, who is leaning into his wife, pointing to something in his magazine.

Esther considers telling the receptionist, The golden years don't last forever. Or perhaps she should raise her arthritic hand and say, Try writing a funny script about this. Instead, she says, "You sound like my daughter. Ceely's always trying to improve me. Now she thinks I should join a book club."

The receptionist perks up. "A book club would be nice."

"I like to select my own books," Esther says. "I'm reading one of Oprah's books at the moment." She doesn't have the heart to explain that she has few friends left, and most of them have moved away. To Florida. Arizona. Shirley Levine and her husband are in Santa Fe. Once a year they visit Chicago, she with her turquoise and silver, he with his leather vest. There is Lorraine, of course. But two hardly constitutes a group. If she counts Helen Pearlman, that would make three. But Helen is tucked away at Cedar Shores talking nonsense.

The man looks up from his magazine and Esther fears he is about to tell them to pipe down, but then he retreats to his magazine. Marty used to hide behind the newspaper when Esther was talking. If she kept on with her stories, sometimes he'd hold out his hand and pretend to be hitting the mute button on the remote control. She flinches at the memory, surprised at its power to sting after all these years. Then, as if in opposition to the memory, she raises her voice. "Last week, my daughter told me about a tai chi class for seniors." She looks at the man, but when he shows no sign of irritation, Esther wonders if he's hard of hearing.

"And she's trying to get me to move," Esther continues. "But I like it where I am. I tell her the neighbors are good to me. And she says, 'You'll make new neighbors.' Then she shows me a brochure." Esther imagines the silver-haired couple on the cover twirling around a dance floor, dipping and diving. Showing off. But nobody at Cedar Shores looks that good. "You know what they call it?"

"Call what?" The receptionist plucks a moist paper towel from a plastic container and begins wiping down her phone.

"The place where my daughter wants me to move."

The receptionist shrugs as she works the towel into the phone's nooks and crannies.

"They call it 'a concept,'" Esther says, with an ironic smile. "'A new concept in senior living.' That's what the brochure says. There's a picture of a couple with silver hair. They're on a sofa. Just the two of them. They're drinking wine. Nobody in the brochure is shuffling around in walkers, or slumped over in wheelchairs."

The receptionist nods. "Maybe your daughter has a point."

"So you think I should be in that place?"

"No!" The man leans forward, as if he's about to fly out of his chair. "Don't go. Trust me. They put my brother in one of those places. His daughter showed him all the brochures." He waves his magazine in the air, as if it were the very brochure that had caused his brother's undoing. "She took him there for a tour, and after he got back he called me and said he'd rather die. Before he moved in, they held some shindig for newcomers. Everybody got a bottle of champagne." He turned to his wife. "Remember, Millie?" She holds out her magnifier as if it might possibly double as a memory aid. Then she slips back into her magazine. "It was all smoke and mirrors," the man says. He leans over and taps Millie on the knee. "Remember, that baloney about a concierge?" Millie nods, but Esther can tell she doesn't have a clue. And then, visibly dispirited by Millie's inability to corroborate his story, the man sinks back into his chair without finishing his tale.

Esther is about to encourage him to continue, when the receptionist, sounding annoyed that their conversation had been hijacked by the man, says, "I meant the tai chi, Mrs. Lustig. Or that book group. Maybe your daughter has a point about that." Brightening, she says, "Or dancing."

Esther glances down at her feet and thinks of the house slippers awaiting them at the side of her bed. "No," she says, shaking her head. "I don't think so."

By the time Esther arrives home she has forgotten her intention to sew the button back on her coat. Instead, she changes into her blue dress, then lies down on top of the chenille bedspread and tries recalling the yoga pose Sophie taught her. The corpse pose. What a name. Esther places her arms loosely at her sides, lets her legs relax, and closes her eyes. If she's lucky, this is how she'll appear when they find her—faceup, arms at ease, inert but composed. "Still life on chenille bedspread," she whispers. "Still life."

But what if she lingers like Miss Smaller, who will be remembered at Devonshire Arms by the stench of decay she left behind? She consoles herself with the thought that Miss Smaller died in August, during the dog days. Perhaps Esther will make her exit in January, with the heat turned low. She read once that a famous impressionist, she can't remember which one, had worked in a cold studio to extend the life of the fruit he was painting. Now his canvases fetch millions. What was his name? Marty would remember. He remembered things like that, the things she did not. And she remembered for him. Together, she supposed, they'd made a whole person.

She runs her hand across the silky blue, amazed at how much pleasure it still gives her. Mrs. Singh did a beautiful job with the alterations. Alberta, at Ziegler's, couldn't have done better. Before Esther's hands—what useless claws!—betrayed her, she could have fixed the dress. Mrs. Rothstein, her father's seamstress, had taught her well. Oh, how she'd sewed! Pinafores for Ceely. Sailor suits and rompers for Barry. Nightgowns and beach cover-ups. Halloween costumes. Ceely's prom dress. Esther fell asleep trying to recall all the fabric that had sailed through her hands.

She dreamed she was altering her blue dress but couldn't find her tailor's dummy. After a frantic search she realized Ceely must have taken it, assuming Esther, in her dotage, would never know it was missing. Or perhaps Sophie donated it to the Museum of Science and Industry. She'd roll her eyes and say, "Nobody sews anymore, Nonna. That thing belongs in a museum." Esther had to get to the museum before it closed. But she couldn't find the car keys. She tried to remember where people leave their keys when they start to lose their marbles. She looked in the freezer, the microwave, the medicine cabinet. Then she called for a taxi, but got a recording in Spanish. She hung up, and thought of calling Mr. Volz for the number of his cab company, but she couldn't remember his number. Then she redialed and again got the Spanish recording. She should have learned Spanish. Her parents spoke Yiddish, which she understood but never learned to speak. Esther never wanted to speak anything but English. When she was angry, she mimicked her mother, corrected her pronunciation. "What!" she'd cry. "Wa. Wa. Wa. Wa. Wa. Not vhat!" Oh, she was a monster child. After the museum, she'll go to the cemetery to apologize. Where was her mother buried? She needs to find her mother, tell her that she loved her. Me too, her mother will say, and then Esther will tell her about the Yiddish revival. "People are writing books about Yiddish. They study it. There's even a Yiddish museum on some fancy New England college campus." Esther has to find her mother. Suddenly, she spots the grave, but before she can reach it, she trips on Marty's headstone. "You're here!" she cries. "But where's my plot?" And he tells her, "Don't you remember, Essie? You wanted to be burned." She tells him she was only joking. "Where's my mother, Marty? Where is she?"

A noise startles her awake. Even after she opens her eyes, it takes her a minute to realize she's no longer dreaming. Her granddaughter is standing over her, a look of concern on her face. Esther smiles up at her. "Sophie, darling. I must have fallen asleep," she says, reaching for her granddaughter's hand.

"Nonna." Sophie leans over to kiss Esther's cheek. "Why are you wearing your dress?"

Esther smiles and reaches for Sophie's hand. "What time is it? Is our dinner tonight?"

Sophie shakes her head. "It's tomorrow." She strokes Esther's hand. "I was just driving past and decided to ring the bell. When you didn't answer . . ."

Esther looks at her granddaughter, standing there, her spine easily and beautifully straight. She has hair of ear-lobe length and her father's surprising eyes—one blue, one brown. Yet she has none of Lenny's strong features; she's been spared his myopic eyes. She is a beauty. "It's all right," Esther says, drawing Sophie's hand closer to kiss it. "One of these days it's going to happen. And when it does, you'll see. Everything will be all right."

"I'm glad you're not in such a hurry," Esther says.

"I'm sitting." Ceely sounds peeved. Dramatically, she rises from her chair, then settles back down with a thud. "Now stop complaining."

Esther dunks a teabag in Ceely's cup before placing it in her own. "I'm not complaining."

"Then why did you say that? And why, if this is such a red-letter occasion, don't we get our own tea bags?"

"My mother did the same. You'll see," Esther replies. "We're wired this way." She wraps the tea bag around a spoon to extract any remaining flavor before setting it on her saucer. "Is it possible," she says, "that you're afraid to sit with your old mother?"

"Don't start," Ceely says, with an impatient wave of the hand.

"Maybe." Esther pauses, then stands her ground. "Maybe you're afraid if you sit long enough, I'll ask questions."

"Like what?" Ceely's eyes widen with curiosity. They're pretty eyes, hazel with flecks of green and gold that sparkle in the light.

"I don't know." Esther shrugs. There's so much she could ask. So much that she doesn't know about her daughter. "For starters, I could ask why you ran away."

"Jesus, Ma. That was a million years ago." Ceely purses her lips, like Esther, like Esther's mother. Three peas in a pod, and she doesn't even know it. "Besides. I didn't run away. I just didn't come home for a while. There's a difference."

"A difference? You could have fooled me." Esther wants to lean across the table, brush her daughter's cheek, pat her hand. They've never spoken about Vermont. Confrontation has never been Esther's style, though she always had plenty of lip for Marty. Pursed lips. That's how Esther dealt with disappointment. And once Ceely returned, came back and lived with them for a few months before doing what all the other young people did, getting her own apartment—once she returned, Esther couldn't raise the matter for fear her daughter would take off again. Instead, she threw herself into proving to Ceely that she was right to come home. She baked Ceely's favorite granola cookies, made pots of her favorite lentil soup, carried mugs of herbal tea to her while she camped out at the dining room table translating that inscrutable poetry.

The years passed. Never again did Ceely give them cause for detectives, for tears and recrimination. Yet Esther is always on guard, anticipating another round of the silent treatment, phone calls that go unheeded, mail returned to sender, not that she mails letters to Ceely across town. In all this time, not once has she asked: What happened? Did we do something? Did I do something? What was it? That's four questions. But really, they're all the same.

Now here they are, two women sitting at a kitchen table over cups of tea. Then Esther had to go and break the spell. Why couldn't she keep her mouth shut? Why couldn't she navigate the conversation to safer ground? And why was it so easy talking to other women? Even Mrs. Singh, the other day, stood chattering at the mailbox like a mynah bird. She showed Esther her arm, where it was still tender to the touch, and how it bowed slightly where it hadn't set right in its cast. She informed Esther that Mr. Singh was doing much better. It might be the new medication he was taking; whatever it was, they were planning a vacation. "Maybe we'll go to California this winter." An entire branch of the Singh family lives in Sherman Oaks. Then Esther revealed that her sister had lived in Santa Monica. "I didn't know you had a sister," Mrs. Singh said, and when Esther nodded and explained, Mrs. Singh's eyes welled up and she patted Esther's back as if Esther were just setting out for Anna's funeral. They stood talking like that, one word flowing after the other.

Esther looks across the table at Ceely, wondering what word, if any, might trigger such a flow. Or perhaps they will be locked forever in this uneasy détente, and Esther will never know why Ceely ran away all those years ago. Or why she returned. Or anything else about her life that really matters.

"You know." Esther's voice cracks. She pauses and starts over. "You know."

"Yes?" Ceely leans forward, cocks an eyebrow.

Esther stares into her cup, as if it contained the words that elude her. She recalls telling Lorraine, just the other day, how Ceely and Sophie end their phone calls with, "Love you!" Ceely and Josh, too. "They say it, like I might say to you, 'Tomorrow is your turn to call,'" she told Lorraine. "It's so automatic, I wonder how much it can mean. But it's nice the way they talk to each other. I realized I'd never said that to Ceely. Maybe she thinks I don't love her."

"Maybe revelations of love are not your style," Lorraine told Esther.

"Ma!" A look of concern crosses Ceely's face. "You were saying something?"

Esther, startled into the present, says, "I was going to tell you about Lena. Milo's wife. You've seen her. Long legs. Big red hair. She wears those tall leather boots and big gold earrings?"

Ceely shakes her head. "Milo has a wife?"

"I was sure you'd met her. Anyway, she's moved back in. I saw her from the window. I was looking out and there she was, lugging a suitcase toward their apartment."

"That's what you wanted to tell me?"

Esther nods, but is unable to meet her daughter's gaze. "She moved out about a month ago. Ella Tucker, in 3A, the one I avoid, got hold of me at the mailboxes. She'd heard that Lena had left Milo and moved in with the man who teaches English at the community center. Ella blamed it on Milo's mother. She said, 'That old woman drove Lena right into the arms of another man.' I told Ella I wouldn't know, that I thought I'd seen Lena earlier that day. Ella said, 'No. You wouldn't know.'" Esther looks up, gives her daughter a rueful smile. "Anyway, now you know why I listen for Ella to go down for her mail. Then, when she's done, I go and get mine."

Esther catches Ceely checking her watch. "What's wrong?"

If she'd told this story to Mrs. Singh, the two women would be lost in conversation for the longest time.

"Nothing." Ceely rises and carries her cup to the sink.

"I said something, didn't I?"

"No." Ceely runs the water, then stops. "That's just it, Ma," she says, her voice bristling with frustration. "You didn't say a thing."

"But I just told you a story. What do you want me to say?"

Ceely shrugs. "Listen. I'm late."

Esther holds up a hand. "Wait. Don't go. I have something to show you." She rises and heads slowly to the living room. When she returns, she is clutching an awkward-looking object, which she sets on the table.

"What's that?" Ceely asks.

Esther, surprised, says, "You don't recognize it?"

Ceely considers it through narrowed eyes and shakes her head. "Not really."

"You made it. You must remember."

For a moment they both stare at the mottled brown mug, as if it might suddenly perform a trick or start talking.

Suddenly, Ceely cries out. "Where did you get this!" She reaches for it, turns it over in her hands, runs her fingers over the initials she'd carved into the bottom. "It's pretty awful, isn't it?" She smiles at Esther, then hugs the mug, as if it were the family cat that showed up on the doorstep weeks after everyone thought it had been eaten by coyotes.

Ceely's eyes shine with delight as she turns it over and again runs her fingers over her roughly hewn initials. "I don't understand. How did you get this?"

When Esther carried the mug into the kitchen, she remembered the heat it had given off when Jack handed it to her all those years ago. Jack. She hasn't thought about the detective in ages. She looks at Ceely and understands there are things her daughter doesn't know about her, either.

"It's from the time you ran away," Esther says.

"I told you, I did not run away!" Ceely glares at Esther, the glint in her eyes turning cold.

"When you were away, I drank my tea from it. Every afternoon." Esther holds her daughter's stony gaze. "I'd think, 'Ceely made this with her own two hands.' Holding it was like holding a part of you."

Ceely's face softens. "I can't believe you saved this." She lets out a short laugh, shakes her head. "This may be the ugliest mug I've ever seen." She laughs harder. "I can't believe you ever used it."

"You can believe it," Esther says. Then she checks her watch. "It's getting late. Lenny will be home soon. And Josh. Now get going. You've got things to do."

Over coffee one morning, Esther runs across the obituary of a woman writer who, at the age of seventy-seven, left behind a simple note: I've lived long enough.

Esther, who has already lived eight years longer than the writer, tries the idea out for size. "Enough is enough," she says. But who is there to listen, to argue, to talk her down from the ledge? Certainly not the sugar bowl or the vitamins—what an unlikely pair!—standing mute, like Marty all those years, her words washing over him while he read the paper. The bird isn't much better. Mickey. Dumb bird. Though she is grateful for his chatter. She named him for the parrot that lived in the courtyard of that old hotel in San Miguel. Saint Michael.

Esther wonders if that writer ever sat alone at her table waiting for a sign, for a bird to cry, No!, or for the vitamins to say, Don't be ridiculous! Enough is never enough! And would the sugar bowl nod in agreement?

She laughs at the thought. Sometimes that's all it takes. One laugh and she's down off the ledge. Or Sophie calls to shoot the breeze. Or Lorraine reminds her that they have matinee tickets for a new production at Steppenwolf. And then Esther wants to stick around and see how things turn out.

Yet she can easily imagine the alternative, a day when nobody calls, or she can't laugh at her own jokes, and even the sound of the bird's incessant chatter isn't enough to fill the void.

In the obituary, a friend reports that in recent years the writer had pared down her life. She stopped hosting dinner parties, going to movies, attending the theater, traveling. She stopped fussing over clothes. She tossed out her lipstick; cut her own hair. "Taken all together," the friend observed, "she lived in a room that was too empty."

Esther surveys her kitchen, crammed with stuff: tea tins, an old portable radio, a flashlight, matches, digestive biscuits, cutting board, electric can opener, and a wooden block holding knives she once wielded with a familiar fluency. Potted plants jockey for space on the divider that separates the living room from the kitchen. The room isn't empty at all, but Esther knows that's not what the writer's friend was suggesting. "Maybe it's good to have to go to the grocery store," the friend remarked. Suddenly, Esther remembers the All-Bran that Ceely brought over the other day, though she'd distinctly requested Lucky Charms.


Esther checks her teeth in the rearview mirror, running a finger over them to erase any lipstick smudges. Slowly she pulls away from the curb.

At the first intersection, she turns right to avoid crossing against oncoming traffic. At the next light, she turns right again, and suddenly recalls the year Marty gave her a tennis racket for her birthday, along with a short white dress and socks with pink pom-poms at the heel. She took lessons. She practiced hitting against a backboard. She drove balls into the net, over the baseline, into the next court. "Home run!" she'd cry. "Out of the ballpark!" When Marty accused her of running around her backhand, she said, "Tennis just isn't my game." And for once, he didn't put up a fight.

The Jewel is up ahead on the right. Esther slows down, signals, pulls into the lot, and after cutting the engine, she lets out a sigh. "I made it," she whispers, then sinks back and rests her head on the seat. When she closes her eyes she sees Ceely's importuning hand, waiting for the keys. She sees Dr. Levenson, glowing with sunshine, shaking his head. They want to take away the keys, but she did just fine.

She opens her eyes, sits up straight, but still can't shake a growing sense of unease. What is she doing here among all these cars, all these people dashing into the store, then rushing back to their cars, their carts brimming with groceries, their days just as jammed with plans and obligations? She feels haunted by a failure of imagination. She could have gone to the Art Institute to admire the impressionists, or to Marshall Field's to linger at the perfume bar, spritz her wrists with the latest scent. She could have walked to the park and sat on a bench.

Esther is about to drive off, when there's a tap on the window. A woman, about Ceely's age, is peering in, her hand shading her eyes as if she were scouting intruders on the horizon. She's wearing a severe black suit and pearls. Her haircut, like Ceely's, is expensive. Tentatively, Esther rolls down the window, letting in a rush of perfume.

"Are you all right?" The woman crouches, bringing herself eye level with Esther.

"I'm fine," Esther says, without conviction.

"Oh." The woman frowns as if to convince Esther that she might not be fine. "You were sitting there for such a long time, I just wondered." She cocks her head to one side, the way one might express sympathy to a child who has just scraped her knee.

"I appreciate your concern," Esther says. "But I'm okay. Really. Thank you." She pulls the keys from the ignition and when the woman shows no signs of leaving, Esther says, "I was just making a shopping list."

At that, the woman presses closer and peers inside the car.

"A mental list," Esther says, defensively.

"Oh." The woman, her good intentions thwarted by this obstinate woman, sounds disappointed. "Well, do you need any help?"

"With a list?" Esther smiles ruefully at the stranger. For years, she scoured the newspaper ads, clipped coupons, made lists of all the specials. Even when she no longer needed to economize, she went from store to store for the door busters. It was a game and she was good at it. The ball always went over the net. She never had to run around her backhand or plot a route that avoided left-hand turns. It's what she did. "I should say not," she declares.

"I thought," the woman stammers. "I thought you looked a bit lost."

"Well, I'm not." Then, with as much dignity as she can muster, Esther drops her keys into her purse and snaps it shut.

Esther grabs a shopping cart and makes a beeline for the cereal aisle where she sets two cartons of Lucky Charms in her basket. But when she envisions Ceely bustling about her kitchen after the funeral, dumping the Lucky Charms into a garbage bag, she sets one back. Dr. Levenson, with his vacation plans, can stock up on cereal, she thinks, as she proceeds down the aisle.

Briefly, she stops to inspect a display of roasted chickens that are warming under heat lamps. They remind her of the man on the radio who said, "Cooking is over." When she heard him, she thought she'd mistakenly tuned in to one of those wild talk shows where conspiracy theories abound. But then the familiar velvety voice of her favorite radio host interrupted with some smart rejoinder before asking listeners to phone in. Esther considered calling in to describe Mrs. Singh's curries and chapatis, and her sister-in-law Clara's kugels. Cooking is over. What a theory! Now, looking at those chickens, lined up

like premature babies asleep under grow lights, she acknowledges the man's point.

Esther and her mother used to walk to the poultry market
on Kedzie Avenue. Esther pushed Ceely in the stroller while her
mother warned her to slow down, watch the uneven sidewalks,
go gently over the curbs, look both ways before crossing. "Next
week, you can go alone," threatened Esther, who couldn't afford
a kosher chicken and was there to escort her mother the eight
blocks from home. Mrs. Glass, who grew flustered and agitated
when English failed her, never left home alone.

The poultry market reeked of singed feathers and warm
blood. It rang with the shrieks of chickens stacked floor to ceiling in wooden cages. The birds clucked and cried and flapped
their wings, raining feathers down on the sawdust-covered floor.

Recently, Esther described the scene to Sophie, who was as
religious in her devotion to fresh food as Esther's parents had
been to Jewish dietary law. Sophie only eats birds that have run
free and been fed nothing but grub worms, nuts, and the seeds
from native plants. She further restricts her diet to food grown
within a fifty-mile radius.

"Those were the days," Esther said, when she told her granddaughter about their excursions down Kedzie Avenue. "Three
generations. All together," she sighed, glossing over Mrs. Glass's
annoying instructions. "It was nice," she told Sophie, as she poured
their tea. After slicing two pieces of apple cake, Esther paused, as
though stopping to admire a painting that has caught her eye.

Sophie urged her on. "What happened to the store, Nonna?"

"Who knows?" Esther shrugged. "We moved. Like everybody in those days. We left the city. The Koreans moved in. Then
the Indians. And now the young people, like you, flocking back
to the place their parents and grandparents couldn't wait to flee."

"And you, Nonna. You came back."

Esther smiled. "I suppose I did." She paused. "But it isn't the same."

Nothing's the same, Esther thinks, as she passes the roasted chickens. Cooking is over.

At the deli, she is cheered by the array of prepared salads, wedges of cheese, slabs of processed meats. Behind the counter, a baby-faced young man with pink cheeks is holding up a slice of Swiss cheese. "Like this?" he mouths to a woman who is talking on her mobile phone. She nods and keeps talking. "Then I go out on the porch and there's all these potted plants," she is saying. "It looks like a frigging greenhouse. There's a note with my name on an envelope. In Brad's writing."

The woman pauses long enough to consider a slice of ham the clerk is holding up. She shakes her head and indicates with her fingers the desired thickness, before returning to her call.

Esther is torn between finding out what was in Brad's note and telling the woman to pipe down, that everybody can hear her business. Her mother used to move through the house, shutting windows at the first sign of an argument. "The neighbors will hear," she would hiss.

But the clerk smiles cheerfully as he hands the ham to the woman. When she walks off, the phone still pressed to her ear, Esther has an urge to follow, tell her to get back and thank the young man. She feels a tap on her shoulder. "You're next," someone says.

"Me?" Esther looks up at the smiling clerk and is seized by a sudden and overwhelming panic. Who is this young man with the baby face? Once she knew all the clerks, joked with them, called them by name. Tony used to run to the back for the best strawberries. The butcher saved the choicest cuts of meat for her. Then he retired, and Tony had a heart attack, collapsed right into a pyramid of Georgia peaches.

I'm living among strangers, she thinks as she studies the clerk's pink face. "Ma'am?" A look of concern clouds his features. "Are you all right?"

Why does everyone keep asking that? She still can't shake the encounter in the parking lot with that woman peering into the car. She feels tired. Well, who wouldn't, when some total stranger comes up and asks if you're all right, as if you were crossing a busy intersection with a white cane or standing in the middle of a sidewalk reading a map? The thought that she looked as helpless as a blind woman or a disoriented tourist fills her with shame. And now this clerk, who is no older than her grandson, is questioning her state of being.

Esther manages a joke, tells the young man she'd been so engrossed in the woman's phone call that she forgot what she wanted. "By the way," Esther says. "She should have thanked you."

The young man leans across the deli case, and though he isn't quite shouting, he articulates every word, the way Esther does when speaking to Milo. "Have you decided what you want?"

If she were to tell him, would he believe her? She wants one more morning with Marty beside her in bed. She wants to wake up each morning with a sense of purpose. She wants her daughter to stop pushing brochures on her. She wants her son to straighten up and fly right. She wants to be something other than the object of concerned looks and condescension.

The clerk is waiting for her to speak. She should say something. She feels in her coat pocket, as if she might discover a list, but all she finds is an old tissue. And a button. She still hasn't sewn it back on. If she had remembered to do that, or if she'd dressed up a bit, perhaps she might not arouse such concern. Her mother wore a Persian lamb coat when she left home. She was a short woman who stood tall. She carried herself with dignity.

"Ma'am?" The clerk is growing impatient.

Esther points to the display case. "I'll have some of that. The smoked salmon," she says. "One slice, please." Then she pauses. Should she explain that she can afford more, but since Marty died she has little reason to cook? In the evening, she scrambles an egg or spreads peanut butter or goat cheese on toast. "Okay. Two slices," she says. "If you don't mind."

"Why would I mind?" His face clouds with confusion. "You can have whatever you want."

Whatever she wants. When was the last time she did that? For years, she did what Marty wanted, or the children. Even today, when she could have visited the Art Institute, a park, or even Marshall Field's, she came here as if she still had a household to feed, as if her destiny was to spend a lifetime pushing a cart up and down the aisles of a supermarket. She hates to think of all the hours she's logged here. Walk away. Now. Go to the park. Look at some paintings. But the young man is waiting, more patiently than Marty ever did. "Stop," she'd tell Marty, as they neared the store. "We're out of milk. I'll just be a minute." He'd pull into the lot, leave the motor running as she hopped out of the car. By the time she returned, he was pounding the steering wheel, fuming and shouting. "What took you so long?"

She looks up at the young clerk. His baby-pink face is open to her, waiting, as if he had all the time in the world. "Some of that, too," she says, her bent finger pointing to the rice pudding.

In the juice section, Esther recalls that this is where Milo's mother broke down on her first outing to the supermarket. Milo had removed his Cubs cap and stopped sweeping the front walk to tell Esther about the call he'd received from the store manager. "Too many orange juice," he said, as if that were a reasonable cause for a meltdown in a grocery store. Now Esther sees the display through Mrs. Belic's eyes. Orange juice with pulp. Without pulp. Fortified with calcium. Laced with vitamin C. Blended with grapefruit. Yogurt, too! In Belgrade, before Mrs. Belic fled, a single orange would have been cause for celebration. "My mother," Milo told Esther. "She didn't know what to do with too many orange juice." Now his mother, who for years had been an administrative assistant at a distinguished university, won't leave the apartment.

When had life morphed so out of control? Esther's mother squeezed oranges by hand. Then came juice in bottles and wax cartons. Frozen concentrate had seemed like an improvement at the time. Now there was all this. Too many orange juice. So this is what happens while you're living your life. Stuff accumulates. Then why does she feel so empty?

She pictures the lines running through the names in her address book, darkening its pages. Mentally, she draws a line through the butcher and Tony and the poultry market on Kedzie. Was this why we had all these choices? To balance the losses? To make us forget that every day our lives become a little less full than they were the day before? Still. Esther can't imagine being consoled by a carton of orange juice with extra pulp.

At the checkout, Esther unloads her cart. Once, she filled the carts to overflowing. When did she become a woman who could easily stand in the express line? But she's not in a rush; nobody is waiting for her. She prefers to blend in with the people whose carts suggest children under foot, company for dinner, lunch-boxes to be packed, and midnight raids on the pantry.

The checker finishes up a large order and without looking up, starts to scan Esther's groceries. Esther leans in toward her and smiles. Dawn G.? She can barely make out her name tag.

Once Esther knew all the checkers by name. She'd been in-volved in their lives same as she'd been with the soap opera heroines she followed while Ceely and Barry napped. Not that Edna or Sharon led particularly dramatic lives, but there had been a few cliff hangers over the years: a husband's layoff, a daughter jilted at the altar, a premature baby, brushes with cancer. Through it all, those women smiled whenever Esther appeared at their register, which she selected over all the others, because they never made mistakes, not even when they had to punch in the price of every item.

"I bet that's uncomfortable," she says, pointing to the brace on Dawn G.'s wrist.

"Carpal tunnel." Dawn G. extends her arm, as if flaunting an engagement ring. "It's from repetitive stress." To demonstrate, she scans the bar code on the Lucky Charms.

Esther holds up a hand, hoping to console Dawn with her own infirmity. The joints closest to the fingertips are frozen in place, permanently bent toward the palm, while the joints nearest the palm flare out.

"Eeeyoooo." Dawn makes a face.

"It's from arthritis," Esther says, quickly withdrawing the offending hand. "The doctor calls it a swan's neck deformity."

Dawn's face softens. Without the silver stud, which has inflamed her lower lip, she would be quite pretty. "Sounds better than it looks," she says. "Does it hurt?"

"Probably not as much as your wrist." Esther pauses, wondering how to explain. "But there are things I can't do anymore."

"Like what?"

"Chopsticks, for one."

"I suppose that's not so bad." Dawn shrugs. "I mean, I could live without chopsticks."

Esther doesn't tell Dawn that she also lives without lacing her walking shoes (she's switched to Velcro), or clasping a necklace (she wears long beads), or buckling her watch (she wears Marty's old Timex with the expandable band). Soon, she will have to live without a car. (She makes a mental note to call Fanny Pearlman for a ride to the cemetery.) It's true. She can live with these accommodations. It's the accretion of them that wears her down and the fear that someday she'll be rendered inoperable, like the stove she once used, even after the right burner went out, and the timer broke, and the self-cleaning element went kerflooey. She used that stove until one day the whole thing conked out.

Suddenly, there is shouting. "I'm not letting you go alone. And that's that!" The woman with the phone is standing directly behind Esther, making no effort to lower her voice. "I've got enough on my mind. I don't need to worry about you running around, God knows where. So read my lips. N.O."

Esther reads her lips, surprised that she hadn't noticed them earlier. They're plumped up, like an overcooked hotdog. She remembers when Lorraine had her eyes done and looked Chinese for a year. Then one day she looked like Lorraine, and Esther told her she'd be crazy to do that again.

"What are you staring at?" The woman glares at Esther. "No, not you," she shouts into the phone. "I was talking to the old lady in front of me."

Abruptly, Esther turns to Dawn. "Tell me something," she says. "Do you mind when people are on the phone while you're checking their orders?"

Dawn shakes her head. "Nah."

"But it's as if you're not there. Invisible."

Dawn shrugs.

Esther understands that if she'd been on the phone all those years, she never would have known that Edna's granddaughter went into labor on the day of her high school graduation, or that Sharon's daughter had been a cutter. You don't learn such things if you're on the phone. And when Marty was sick, Esther would tell them, "He's holding up." No need to go into detail. "Well, you take care of yourself, Esther," they'd say.

She remembers telling Marty that Sharon's husband had a stroke. When she told him that Mrs. Ziegler at the dry cleaners didn't know if she'd ever take another vacation, because she lost her sister and Mr. Ziegler refused to travel, Marty said, "You should work for the FBI, Essie." Sometimes he'd say, "How do you extract so much information?" And she'd say, "Doesn't everyone?" When he'd say, "I don't," she'd reply: "You'll find, Marty, that if you talk to someone, they'll talk back. Isn't that what it's all about?"

Esther turns and faces the loud woman. "Excuse me," she calls out.

But the woman goes right on yakking.

"Excuse me." Esther raises her voice, but it's trembling.

The woman scowls, then turns her back to Esther.

"Perhaps you didn't know that your voice travels." Now Esther is shouting. "We can hear every word. I thought that if you knew . . ."

Suddenly, the woman pivots and casts a menacing look at Esther, who is about to suggest that she continue her call outside or, at the very least, lower her voice. But she can only see those frankfurter lips moving to their own beat and the next thing Esther knows, she's ramming her cart into the woman's cart, which strikes the woman's hip and knocks her off balance.

"What the fuck!" the woman cries. Then, into the phone, "I'll call you right back."

A bead of perspiration breaks out on Esther's upper lip. Her heart feels poised to burst through her blouse, pop the buttons right off. Please, God. Not here. Don't let me die here. Not in front of strangers. Then her knees begin knocking and she leans into her cart for support. Somehow she manages to turn back to Dawn, who is still scanning the groceries as if such disturbances break out in her line every day.

"How's that wrist holding up?" Esther asks, struggling to hide the tremor in her voice.

Dawn replies with a frown and a brief flick of her wrist as she finishes Esther's order.

Esther is trying to make sense of Dawn's indifference, her lack of curiosity—a steady diet of television? too many years spent in day care?—when a sharp pain courses through her hip. Again, she wonders if she's having a heart attack, though she'd always expected to feel a stabbing ache in her chest or upper arm. She is seized by another sharp pain, this one accompanied by the cell phone woman shouting, "I'm talking to you!" Then Esther feels another blow as the woman rams the cart again and screams, "What the fuck did you do that for?"

Esther rubs her hip, pretending to ignore the woman. She wishes Dawn G., who is bagging the groceries with that gimpy hand, would step on the gas.

Meanwhile, hot dog lips is demanding to speak to the manager. "Where is he? Will somebody please call the manager?"

"Why don't you call him yourself?" Esther blurts. "On that stupid phone of yours."

"What did you say?" Now the woman is standing at the front of Esther's cart, while dopey, indifferent Dawn bags the groceries as if she were handling quails' eggs or peaches that cost five dollars a pound. Esther's heart is racing so out of control that she's sure she's about to die. Right here in the checkout line. At least Mrs. Belic was escorted out of the store on her own two feet. But Esther pictures being carted away on a stretcher in a ratty old coat with a missing button. What was she thinking, leaving the house in this old coat? An old lady, isn't that what the cell phone lady had called her? An old lady. A worn out lady in a worn out coat. Again, she recalls her mother, parading up and down the aisles in her Persian lamb. Odd, too, since Mrs. Glass had encased every stick of living room furniture in plastic. Yet she wore that fur coat like there was no tomorrow.

"What did you say?" The woman is glaring at Esther. "I'm talking to you, you old bat," she cries.

"Old bat?" Esther steadies herself with her cart. "Old bat? You think you'll never be old? You can plump those lips all you want, but you'll still wear out like the rest of us." Esther is going to die right here in her old black coat, and she doesn't care. She feels fearless, reckless, and at the same time, eerily calm, as if she were standing in the eye of her own storm. "You want to know what I said?" She glares back at the woman. "I said, 'Call him yourself.'"

"What appears to be the problem?" The manager, a chubby young man in a short-sleeved white shirt and black string tie is at the rude woman's side, and then he is leading her to his cubicle at the other end of the store.

Esther's hand shakes as she opens her wallet. "I don't know what came over me," she tells Dawn. "You have to believe me. I've never done anything like that before." She hands over exact change. "If Edna were here, she'd tell you. Or Sharon. They'd vouch for me."

Late afternoon light streams through the bedroom window, revealing the ceiling crack for what it really is. It isn't a line snaking across a map. It isn't the mighty Mississippi or the lesser Chicago. It's a cracked ceiling in need of repair. "Like me," says Esther, who is lying in bed staring up at it. She holds up her crooked hand, studies it from this angle and that, knowing it is beyond repair, yet hoping that it might have changed since she last saw it into something useful—a hand that can manage shoelaces, chopsticks, buttons.

Her coat is on. She can't remember ever climbing into bed in her clothes. Not even for a nap. Yet somehow she'd stumbled into bed fully clothed and passed out. Like a drunk.

The mid-October days are growing shorter, but there is still enough light to see how frayed the cuff is. Last winter, Ceely phoned about a sale at Marshall Field's. "I'll look into that," Esther promised, though she had no intention of buying a coat that would end up at Goodwill before she had time to break it in.

She tells herself to get up, take the coat off, put the groceries away. She starts to rise, but pauses to tug at a loose thread on the cuff. The afternoon comes rushing back: the awful woman shouting at her; indifferent, oblivious Dawn; her own anxiety, masquerading as a heart attack. How pitiful she must have looked in this old coat. Who would know—not Dawn, not the pudgy manager, certainly not that wretched woman with the phone—that she possessed finer garments (even this coat was stylish once), or that her father had been the proprietor of a women's dress and fur shop? Closing her eyes, she sees the candies he set out in a cut-glass dish beside the register. She can see the look of pleasure on his face the time he surprised her mother with a mink, the coat that hung in her sister-in-law Clara's closet, causing Esther so much heartbreak.

After Mrs. Glass died, Clara delivered the coat to Esther. "It's yours," she said. Esther unzipped the garment bag and slipped the coat off its cedar hanger. She tried the coat on. The sleeves were too short; the hem didn't reach to her knees. She set the coat back in the bag and hung it in her closet, where it shared space with a jumble of garments, some of which Esther had been meaning to send to Goodwill.

When Esther went off to college, her father gave her a mouton coat. But first, he made her put it on and parade up and down State Street, while carrying a sign that advertised his shop. It was the dog days of August, and when she protested, her father said, "Esther, let this be a lesson for you. No lunch is for free." Oh, how she cried.

Now she parades around in a frayed coat with a missing button. Why? And why did she ram her cart into that wretched woman and make such a scene? Who would believe that Frank used to run to the back for fresh strawberries? Or the butcher—she can't recall his name, but she still can see the gap between his front teeth when he smiled—steered her away from the meat that had been standing out too long? Who would believe that she knew how Edna's daughter was jilted at the altar, or that Sharon's husband had that stroke and couldn't move his toes for a week and then all of a sudden he could?

Esther flings an arm over her eyes, trying to blot out the memory of the day's misadventures. Then another memory surfaces, one that involves her mother, in yet another checkout line.

Before Esther's mother moved to Miami Beach, where the only downside, as Mrs. Glass liked to say, was that it was too hot for her mink, the two women shopped for groceries on the day the weekly specials appeared in the *Sun-Times*. Esther drove and her mother, who didn't possess a license, directed Esther, as if driving were something that could be managed by remote control. By the time the women reached the A&P, which was always the first stop in their rounds of the supermarkets (they went from store to store taking advantage of the specials), Esther was ready to push her mother into the path of the first oncoming shopping cart.

Though each woman arrived with a separate shopping list, there were always unexpected temptations: two quarts of strawberries for the price of one; buy one pound of Italian plums, get the second pound free. Concessions were made when only one of them desired a particular two-for-one item. But should both women agree that, yes, strawberries would be nice, they still had to decide who would pay the extra penny for the odd-priced goods.

One day, while standing in line at the register, Mrs. Glass pulled a slip of paper from her purse and started jotting numbers with a stubby pencil. Looking up at her daughter, she said, "I paid the extra penny for the Thompson grapes last week. The ones that were two pounds for ninety-nine cents at Jewel." To dispel any doubt, she handed the chit to Esther.

Right there, in the checkout line at the A&P, Esther wadded the paper into a ball, stuffed it in her mouth and swallowed. Then she handed her mother two pennies, one for the grapes and the other for the peaches that were still in their carts. Mrs. Glass accepted the coins as if they were gold bullion. After dropping them in her purse, she said, in the same even tones she'd used to remark on the weather, "Please, Esther, you're making a scene."

Now, staring at the ceiling, Esther says, "You made some

scene today, didn't you, Esther?" Then she rolls over and faces Marty's side of the bed. She strokes the pillow where his head used to lay and imagines him saying, *The woman had it coming, Essie. Really, you were great.*

That would be quite a compliment, coming from Marty. She sighs, knowing he never would have consoled her, and Esther feels her indignation rising again. The woman did have it coming. She lacked the courtesy to conduct her business in private. What's more, she lacked the good sense to understand how our lives are enriched by the minor interactions that present themselves every day. "Like little gifts," Esther says, rolling away from Marty's pillow and onto her back. "They practically fall into our laps. If we're open to them," she says, addressing the crack in the ceiling.

Yet in one afternoon Esther managed to wipe out a lifetime of goodwill. One shove of the grocery cart and she was finished, toast, kaput, like Milo's mother weeping over too many orange juice.

The phone jars Esther awake. She fumbles with the receiver. "Hello?"

"Good morning," Lorraine chirps.

"Morning?" Esther looks around. Light streams through the window. "What time is it?"

"The usual."

"The usual?"

"Eight-thirty." Lorraine sounds vexed.

"Eight-thirty?" Esther sees that she's still wearing her coat. She tugs at the stubborn thread and recalls again the scene in the supermarket.

"Esther, are you all right?"

Esther nods.

"Esther? Speak to me."

"What do you want me to say?" She unravels more thread.

"I don't know," Lorraine says, with concern. "Say that you're all right."

"I'm all right," Esther says, without conviction.

"You don't sound all right."

"Well, I am," Esther declares. "In fact, I'd better get cracking." Suddenly, she hears her mother impatiently telling her to run in the street, hit her head against the wall, do anything except mope around and be a pest. "I've got things to do," Esther says.

"What things?"

"Things."

"Well, if you want to be that way about it."

"What way?"

"Secretive."

"Oh, Lorraine. I just woke up. I've got a loose thread on my coat."

"Your coat?"

"Is there an echo in this room?"

"You're not making any sense."

Esther considers explaining. Instead, she says, "I'm sorry if you're having trouble understanding." She pauses. "Let's talk later. Maybe I'll make sense after I brush my glasses and put on my teeth."

They laugh at the stale joke.

After hanging up, Esther gives the thread one last tug and it's out.

First Sophie arrives. Then Amos shows up carrying a bicycle wheel. He holds it out, as if he's come bearing flowers. "Where should I set this, Esther?"

She bristles at his informality. If only he'd given her the chance to say, "Call me Esther. Please."

Sophie, who is setting the table, looks up and smiles at Amos. "Hey!" she says. And when he smiles back at her, repeating the greeting, Esther wonders how one word can be so erotically charged. She recalls that the first time Ceely brought Lenny home for dinner, he choked on the roast beef. Esther had hoped her daughter would come to her senses, find a man who didn't wolf his food, talk with his mouth full, someone whose self-confidence put others at ease, a man at home in the world. Yet Esther has come to appreciate her son-in-law, even championed Lenny's cause that time Ceely made noises about leaving. Esther supposes that this Amos, who is wearing a yellow helmet and orange backpack and has all the mannerisms of a rambunctious family dog, and who, her granddaughter has informed her, works in a bakery, though he is really a lawyer, she supposes he could grow on her, too.

Esther's parents had an arranged marriage, though her mother made no secret that as a young woman she'd been in love with another man—the Bondit, she'd called him, invoking his name perhaps at times when her own marriage felt tired or disappointing. What had the Bondit looked like? What had he

159

done? How had they met? Esther never asked. To ask would have felt like a betrayal of her father. Even if she'd asked, her mother might not have remembered. Over time, the Bondit's looks, preferences, mannerisms would have faded in Mrs. Glass's mind, until all that remained was a name, one that left Esther conjuring her mother's first love as a cross between Jesse James and the Cisco Kid. The Bondit sounded dangerous, so unlike her father, whom Esther adored, but who had all the dash and swagger of a women's dress shop proprietor, which is what he was. When Esther was younger, she'd felt heartbroken over her mother's lost love. As an adult she was outraged by a custom that thwarted love for the cold economic motivations of tribal elders. Yet her mother had adored her father. And he worshipped her. Esther couldn't say how she knew. It would have been easier to explain the swallows returning to Capistrano.

If only Esther could arrange a marriage for her granddaughter, she thinks, as she tells Amos to set the tire against the wall.

He removes his helmet, revealing a mop of rust-colored hair, which he makes no effort to rearrange. And when he slips off his backpack she sees that he is wearing a striped T-shirt, the kind she dressed Barry in as a young boy. In his toddler's apparel, Amos's hands and feet appear disproportionately large. Esther looks away to avoid thinking of those overgrown appendages in bed with her golden granddaughter.

Suddenly, the bird lets out a shriek. "Pipe down, Mickey!" Esther cries, though secretly she is grateful for the distraction. When the bird doesn't let up, Amos pokes a finger into its cage and speaks in soothing tones about a bomb that had gone off in a Baghdad market that day. "Two brothers left home in the morning to buy a bird," he coos. "Probably one very much like you."

As the parakeet hops onto Amos's finger, Sophie shrugs and Esther smiles and strokes her granddaughter's cheek.

At dinner, Esther ladles barley-bean soup into white porcelain bowls while Amos, voluble as the bird, chatters about his renunciation of red meat. "E. coli is only part of it. These days, you can get sick from spinach," he declares. "Or tomatoes!" He speaks knowledgeably about the conversion of rain forest to grazing land and about overcrowding in cattle feedlots. He talks about animal waste running off into rivers and streams.

Esther nods, rapt, as if she hasn't heard any of this before. It is the passion with which Amos speaks that captivates her. She is still nodding when he starts talking about cows unleashing methane into the atmosphere. "Ninety-five percent of their gaseous output comes from belching," he says, at which point Sophie sets down her spoon with a clang.

"Amos!"

"What?" He looks confused.

"Nonna doesn't need to hear this."

"That's not true," Esther says, inclining her head toward her granddaughter's boyfriend, who sits wedged between the two of them at the small kitchen table. "I knew about E. coli. Mad cow, too." She pauses. "But all those emissions? That's a whole new angle. In fact, it never occurred to me that cows do." Again she pauses. Having been schooled in the notion that certain topics are off-limits at the dinner table, she wonders how to phrase what comes next. "It never occurred to me that cows . . . that cows." She stops and starts, pausing several times before saying, "That cows . . . that cows belch." There! She said it. And nothing happened. Well, not nothing. She feels carefree and buoyant. Younger.

And then she smiles, which is all the encouragement Amos needs to continue his discourse on the ecological disaster spawned by, as he puts it, "Our insatiable demand for Big Macs."

"Amos, please," Sophie sighs, giving him a fondly disapproving look. "This is hardly dinner talk." Then she turns to seek her grandmother's approval. But Esther's gaze is fixed on Amos. "This is fascinating," she says, leaning closer to Amos and stroking the base of his wine glass. "Don't stop."

"Do stop!" Sophie cries, clapping her hands to her ears. "Please. Can't we please change the subject?"

Amos holds up his hands in mock resignation. "I guess that's enough of that," he declares, grinning at Esther.

She leans over until their shoulders are touching and in a stage whisper says, "I'm certainly glad we're having chicken tonight."

Amos laughs. "I hope it was a happy chicken, Esther."

This time, she doesn't bristle at the sound of her name. "Happy chicken? Why should a chicken be happy?"

"Oh, Nonna," Sophie whines. "Not that." She glares at Esther with those mismatched eyes—her father's eyes.

"Not what?" Amos turns from one woman to the other, grinning, exposing perfect teeth, big teeth, overgrown as his hands and feet. Once again, Esther forces herself to think of something other than Amos in bed with her granddaughter. "Not what?" he repeats.

"Oh, nothing," Sophie snaps.

"Something," he says.

Sophie, who translates poems from Italian into English for a former professor whom Esther suspects she'd slept with, grudgingly acts as interpreter. "My Nonna doesn't think anyone is really happy. 'Who's happy?' It's like her mantra." She turns to Esther. "Right, Nonna?" Then to Amos, she says, "She'll defy you to name one happy person."

Ignoring the challenge, Amos starts talking about what they already know—that earlier in the day more than forty people had been killed, a hundred wounded, in an Iraqi bird market. "A young pigeon vendor, Ali Ahmed—don't ask me how I remember that—told a reporter that it had been a beautiful day, and people, taking advantage of a lull in the fighting, had flocked to the outdoor market and the last thing Ali remembered, before waking up in the hospital, was seeing bodies of the dead and wounded mixed with the blood of the birds. And feathers. Feathers everywhere."

Esther is wondering whether Amos has considered the incongruence of the bloody bird market and the roasted chicken on the blue ceramic platter in the center of the crowded table, when Sophie, who might have sensed her grandmother's displeasure, hijacks the conversation.

"Speaking of chickens," Sophie says. She goes on to describe the pamphlet on the butcher's counter at the natural foods co-op where she shops. "It says the chickens get to roam about. Or range. I can't remember. Roam. Range. I'm not sure I understand the difference. But the point is . . ." Her face has grown flushed, her eyes bright, like a feverish child's. "The point is they're supposed to be happy. The pamphlet actually calls them happy chickens." Her voice trails off. "Though how would anyone know?" Sophie pauses. "That they're happy, I mean." Then she slumps back in her chair, as if sensing that she just talked herself into a corner.

Esther wants to pat Sophie's hand, console her, explain that it isn't her fault; she's wired to stop conversations. It's a trait she acquired, like her mismatched eyes, from her father. Poor Lenny. He can talk until the cows come home, then go right on talking. On the other hand, he has never talked down to Esther, though lately more and more people do just that, as if age has shrouded her in stupidity.

They eat in silence, the only noise coming from the intermittent clink of cutlery on china and the parakeet's occasional outbursts. The table is so compact there isn't even the need to speak up for the salt to be passed.

Suddenly, Esther feels tired. Perhaps it's the wine, though

she's had just a few sips. She takes another, before breaking the silence. "Chickens are stupid," she declares. "When it rains, they hold their heads up to the heavens, open their beaks, and drown. There's nothing happy about that."

"Turkeys, Nonna," Sophie says, patting Esther's arm.

Esther regards Sophie's hand as if it were a cat walking across the table. She recoils from her granddaughter's touch. "What do turkeys have to do with anything?"

"They drown in the rain," Sophie replies, squeezing Esther's arm for emphasis. "Not chickens."

The young couple exchanges a knowing glance. Is there also a hint of triumph in Sophie's face, the way it opens to Amos, as if to say, I told you she couldn't stay on track for long. And you were so charmed by her.

Esther has the urge to tell them that growing old is one of the most surprising things that has happened to her. She hadn't given it any thought. Then one day, she was eighty-five. She is old. Not just old, but an object of derision, pity. Is there any use explaining that she is still herself—albeit a slower, achier, creakier version of the original?

"Turkey. Chicken," Esther says, trying to control the tremor in her voice. "Big bird. Little bird. What's the difference?" She can tell them that she knows a thing or two about birds. She can remind Sophie again about the poultry market on Kedzie. Instead, she says, "Tell me this: How does anyone know the chicken was happy? Sophie's right. Of all the nonsense." She dismisses the nonsense with a wave of her hand.

Esther considers adding that she would never fall for such a marketing gimmick, never pay extra for a bird just because of a brochure. Perhaps she should reveal that the bird set before them on a blue ceramic platter had, until recently, sat under warming lamps at the Jewel. Then she could joke that in all likelihood they're eating an "unhappy" chicken. Cooking is over!

Sophie, didactic as her father, breaks in and says, "The idea, Nonna, is that the chicken lived well until it died. It was fed properly, and treated humanely, to the end. In other words, it was happy until it died." Clearly pleased with herself, she smiles and says, "You could even say it died a happy death."

Esther observes that the knuckle of the index finger of the hand Sophie is using to cut her chicken is smudged black and blue. A tattoo. How long has it been there? Suddenly she wonders how long Sophie and Amos will be here? She's tired. She's tired of all the talk about death. She's tired of having to prove herself, of having to demonstrate her ability to follow a conversation, even one as inane as this. She's tired from the dinner preparations. Once, she could fix a meal without any effort. Last night, she made do with peanut butter on toast. She's tired of having to engage with a young man who, despite the fact that he's a good talker and enjoys second helpings of everything, hasn't bothered to remove the bicycle clips from his pants and who, in all likelihood, will one day walk out the door with his tire and helmet and break her granddaughter's heart.

"Happy death," Esther snaps. "Sounds like an oxymoron to me."

"Oxymoron?" Amos cocks an eyebrow.

"It means . . ." Esther starts.

"I know what it means, Esther."

For the second time this evening, she bristles at the sound of her name.

"But why," Amos continues, "can't the two be used in conjunction?" Then he launches into another spiel, this time about his plans to die at home. "In my own bed." He speaks of his grandmother, who was tethered to tubes in a noisy hospital room before she died. "She had the roommate from hell. All day long, ringing for pillows, juice, cookies, blankets, ice cream." Amos tells them that each time the roommate hollered for something else, he recited, under his breath, a Buddhist loving-kindness meditation. "But by late afternoon I was at the nurses' station threatening to put a pillow over the old bat's head."

Esther recalls sitting at Marty's bedside, holding his hot, dry hand. Leaning closer, she whispered in his ear. "Let's go to Mexico. Just the two of us. I'll drive. You'll sit back and enjoy the ride." Marty opened his eyes. "It's a long drive, Essie." When he closed his eyes and fell asleep she thought of putting a pillow over his head. Sometimes she imagined putting one over her own head. She had no stomach for guns, not like Peppy Grossman, that fellow who'd worked at her brother's shop. Harry got to work one morning, found Peppy slumped over a desk with a note apologizing for the mess. No. Esther could never use a gun. Or a rope, like that sweet Mia Kelly, from down the block. At the memorial service, when Mia's psychiatrist got up and explained that she'd had an illness as real as leukemia or a deformed heart, Esther thought she couldn't have done that, stand there and face down a gathering of mourners who were probably blaming him for dereliction of duty. It took a lot of nerve standing up there, but not half as much as standing on a chair in the basement with a rope around your neck. No, a pillow sounded just right. Almost like dying in your sleep.

"In my own bed," Amos is saying, as if he'd read Esther's mind. "That's the only way to go."

Esther looks at the couple, so young, so sure of themselves, so full of answers. She wishes for Amos a peaceful ending, but first, a long life, though not, she realizes, eyeing the tire propped against the wall, the yellow helmet on the counter, a life with Sophie.

Every January, Sophie and Esther drive to Waldheim to visit Marty on the anniversary of his death. They bundle up in long silk underwear, wool mufflers, heavy coats, and sheepskin boots. Esther fills a thermos with hot tea. She packs a Ziploc bag with Marty's favorite cookies, two of which she leaves on his grave, in lieu of stones. Afterward, Esther takes Sophie to lunch.

But on this brilliant October day, Fanny Pearlman, Helen's daughter, will drive Esther for an unscheduled visit.

Esther waits for Fanny on the living room sofa, her hands folded in her lap, as if she were in an airport lounge listening for her flight to be called. The living room is crowded with the few familiar furnishings she and Marty moved from the house on Shady Hill Road. She has lived among her things for so long that she's become blind to them. Now she takes them in with the wonder of a stranger happening upon the new and unexpected. She's glad that she's hung on to her mother's pink cut-glass bowl, the ceramic water jug from the market in San Miguel, the bone china teacups that she collected one at a time. Photographs in ornamental frames jockey for space on the tabletops.

A sadness akin to grief overcomes Esther at the thought that Ceely and Sophie might not want any of it, not even the red leather chair that she fell in love with at an estate sale in Winnetka. Her daughter-in-law, who can't buy a flower vase without her decorator, won't want a thing. "I suppose it will all have to go," Esther says to the bird, who chirps agreeably.

When the time comes, when Ceely finally gets her way and hustles her off to Bingoville, Esther supposes she can rescue a few pieces, take with her the Persian carpet, the pink bowl, a few pictures. Helen's room at Cedar Shores has just enough space for a bed and an easy chair. She stores a few knickknacks in the pressed-wood bookcase, along with the boxes of Jell-O she buys on weekly outings to the supermarket. Had Helen once sat like this taking inventory, deciding what to take, what to leave behind? Perhaps somebody decided for her.

Esther's eye falls on a photo of five young women sitting on a stone wall in front of an ivy-covered brick building. She picks it up, absentmindedly polishing the silver frame with the hem of her sweater. There they are, five girls from Albany Park (Esther is the one in the middle), sitting on a stone wall outside a college dorm. All of them are dressed in white T-shirts, rolled-up jeans, shiny penny loafers. They were the Starrlites (the name, a silly conceit). Perhaps the casual attire was a uniform. She can't remember, though she remembers that Brenda Starr never would have been caught wearing jeans and a T-shirt. Brenda favored décolletage and high-heeled shoes. Once, all the Starrlites dyed their hair red, like Brenda's, but unlike their heroine they preferred dressing up in ballet slippers, flowing skirts, and peasant blouses. They flirted with bohemianism, smoked cigarettes, signed petitions. Then one by one they married and had children. Their rebellion erupted, if at all, in mildly quotidian ways, by breaking rank with their mothers. Esther cooked pork; she served meat with dairy. Like the other Starrlites, who'd grown up in homes where the only wine served was sweet and reserved for ceremonial occasions—the Sabbath Kiddush, the yearly seder—Esther served cocktails at dinner parties. She went to French films, traveled to Mexico. One year, she took up the guitar and learned to play "We Shall Overcome." For a while, she smoked a pipe, albeit one with a thimble-sized bowl.

Once, years ago, Esther found Ceely curled up on her bed, sucking on a rope of red licorice as she flipped through old photo albums. "Who's this?" she asked, pointing to the picture of Esther seated among her friends on the stone wall. Esther was about to say, "Why it's me, silly!" But then she glimpsed her reflection in the mirror. Glancing back at the picture, she said, "Humpty Dumpty."

Ceely screwed up her face. "What?"

"Humpty Dumpty. You know. He fell off the wall."

"You're weird," Ceely said.

Esther held out a pile of folded laundry. "Get up," she said. "Take these and put them away in your drawer."

She sets the picture back on the end table and consults Marty's old Timex. The watch is too big and the way it flops on her wrist is mildly annoying. But it's easy to put on and it keeps good time. "Like Marty," she says to the bird. "Annoying, yet dependable."

The bird chirps and Esther checks the time. A few more minutes and the Pearlman girl will ring the bell.

When Esther is buckled up (Fanny refuses to start the car until her passenger is securely fastened), she starts talking about her old friend Sonia Markel. "Your mother knew her." Fanny nods, and Esther continues. "I'd been meaning to call, but something always got in the way, though now I can't tell you what. Then one day, I started calling all the names in my address book. A to Z. When I got to the M's, I couldn't wait to speak to Sonia. But I got Buddy instead. For some reason he thought I was in San Diego. When I told him I was in Chicago, he said, 'Ah, Chicago. I hear it's wonderful,' as if he'd always longed to visit."

Speaking to the back of Fanny's head is getting on Esther's nerves, but Fanny refuses to let her passengers ride up front. "The suicide seat's off limits," she said the first time she steered Esther to the backseat. Esther has known Fanny from day one. She was an easy baby who became a large-boned girl with sturdy hands and a strong laugh. She played field hockey in high school and became a serious golfer in college, which Esther remembers because she used to wish that Ceely, who had been so morose in those days, would take up a sport. Fanny never gave Helen any trouble, though she never married, which caused her mother some distress. In the old days, Fanny would have been labeled a spinster or old maid, but Esther knows that such phrases have gone out of style. For some reason, they no longer apply, perhaps because girls like Fanny (would she ever get over thinking of them as girls?) were no longer the exception. Many of Esther's friends had daughters—bright, pretty, capable young women, with successful careers as teachers, doctors, lawyers—who for one reason or another appear to have forgotten to marry.

Fanny bounces from job to job. She cobbles together a life. On weekends, she plays piano with a band that gets gigs at weddings and bar mitzvahs. Recently, she began a driving service that involves transporting older women with disposable income and lapsed drivers' licenses to the hairdresser, airport, doctor's office.

"What kind of job is that for a Jewish girl?" Esther had said when Clara first recommended Fanny's services.

But Fanny is cheerful and conscientious and surprisingly good company. She maneuvers through traffic with a kind of skill and determination she might have honed on the hockey field.

"You've got to understand," Esther continues. "Buddy's no stranger to this city. His father owned the old Rialto on the West

Side. Buddy worked the concession stand, even on school nights. While the movie ran, his parents played chess in the lobby and he sat on a stool behind the candy counter doing his homework. The next day, he'd come to school smelling of popcorn. Now he pretends not to know Chicago. That's what people do. They forget where they came from."

Fanny nods and a sprig of her unruly mane escapes the grip of a thick plastic barrette. Before Helen went gaga (recently she hit a woman who remarked that she liked the rain), she had a standing appointment at a hair salon in Evanston. Esther considers saying something to Fanny about her mother's hairdresser. Or perhaps she can drop the name of the fellow who cuts Ceely's hair.

"Where was I?" Esther says, as she opens her purse and fishes out a box of Tic Tacs.

"They forget where they came from," Fanny says.

"That's right." Esther leans as far forward as the seat belt allows. She wants to rip it off, park herself up front beside Fanny and say that when her time is up, it's up. But she stays put as she tells Fanny, "Sonia wouldn't forget her origins. Sonia is Buddy's wife. Or was. I suppose that's more accurate. We met in high school, around the same time I met your mother."

Esther leans forward again and taps Fanny on the shoulder. "Stick out your hand."

"I'm driving, Mrs. L.," Fanny protests.

"You can drive with one hand. For a second. Now do as I say."

Reluctantly, Fanny obeys, letting Esther shake a few of the tiny mints into her sturdy palm. "There!" Esther chirps. "Isn't that better?" She clasps her purse shut and settles back for the ride. "Now where was I?"

"Sonia's origins."

"Sonia. Yes. I missed her by six months. All those times I'd thought to call, and I missed her by six months. I know you're wondering how the news could have escaped me. I wondered the same thing, until I realized, who would tell me? There's hardly anyone left."

"People lose touch," Fanny offers.

"But we'd been so close." Esther pauses. "She taught me to smoke. I talked her into bleaching her hair one summer. Sonia served me my first drink, not counting the kiddush wine my father set out on Friday nights." Esther laughs. "We got our periods on the same day."

"Like nuns!"

"Nuns?"

"Go on, Mrs. L."

"Anyway, when Buddy told me about Sonia, I was so rattled, I blurted, 'I'm so glad you're alive!'"

Fanny nods, unleashing another tangle of curls, and again Esther wonders if there's a way to work a good hairdresser into the conversation. Maybe she'll even suggest a little color to brighten things up. Fanny's not too old to find someone. For years, she had a boyfriend who managed a restaurant on Rush Street. Helen once confided that she suspected Ned sold drugs on the side. Helen never approved of Ned, especially after he'd been in the picture for too many years without proposing marriage. Then one day Ned was married to a yoga instructor from the East Bank Club.

Esther continues, "I was mortified."

"Oh, Mrs. Lustig."

"Oh, is right. It was an odd thing to say. But I am glad that Buddy is alive. And I'm glad that he's coming to Chicago. He called back the next day and said he'd like to come for a visit. He hasn't been here in years. He'd like to go to the cemetery to visit his parents. His sister's there, too."

"You're meeting Buddy at the cemetery?"

Esther glares at the back of Fanny's frizzly head. "No! What an idea. Buddy invited me to lunch. But first, I need to speak to Marty. I need him to understand that I want to be out in the world. For a while longer. Then Ceely can stash me away in that mauve-colored joint."

The red leather and warm woods come as a welcome relief from the damp, gray early November day. The Coq d'Or isn't stark, stainless, or cool, like so many of the restaurants that have sprung up around town. Esther took Sophie here after their last visit to the cemetery and throughout the meal endured her granddaughter's sarcastic observations. "You realize we're having lunch in a museum display, Nonna. Like those recreations of old Indian villages? Or cave dwellings? One day, they'll pack this place up and reassemble it at the Museum of Science and Industry." Sophie rolled her eyes and, smiling at her own cleverness, continued. "They'll put it somewhere between the old nickelodeon and Colleen Moore's dollhouse." For the rest of the meal, a dispirited Esther saw everything through her granddaughter's jaundiced eye: the discreet waiters, the long-stemmed water goblets, the crisp napkins, the heavy cutlery, even the tiny cruet of sherry meant to be poured over the restaurant's signature clam chowder. All the little touches that ordinarily brought Esther pleasure had appeared off-kilter. Today, though, she intends to enjoy it all. This restaurant, tucked away below the bustling lobby of the Drake Hotel, is her kind of place. Esther feels as if she's come home.

As her eyes adjust to the muted light, she scans the room for a silver-haired man in a navy-blue blazer. Of course, half the diners fit that bill, but Buddy, lean and tall, good-looking in a Cesar Romero kind of way, is sure to stand out. She remembers that he could wear a mustache without evoking thoughts of Hitler or looking as if something had died on his upper lip.

Suddenly, the maitre d' appears and spirits her to a banquette in a dimly lit corner of the clubby room. He leaves her standing beside a table where an old man is perusing a menu. Esther is about to call out to the maitre d' when the man looks up from his menu and stares at her with the most familiar blue eyes. He studies her intently as if she were a painting he doesn't quite understand. Then he breaks into a smile, and with effort steadies himself on the table and like a long-legged wading bird, unfolds his lanky frame.

"Esther! Esther! It's so good to see you." He moves toward her, arms outspread, like a toddler taking fledgling steps. Esther takes him in. He is wearing a navy-blue blazer, tattersall shirt, and striped tie. Then her eyes travel to his feet, and after seeing that he is wearing gym shoes with Velcro closures, she looks away. Seeing those childish shoes feels like an invasion of this man's privacy.

"Buddy! Buddy Markel!" Cheerfully, she returns the greeting. An awkward exchange of air kisses follows, before he ushers her to the booth and they both settle down.

"There!" he exclaims, beaming at her from across the table. "That wasn't so bad."

She shakes her head and smiles uncertainly. For days, she's practiced saying, "I'd recognize you anywhere," but with the exception of those dazzling blue eyes, there is nothing familiar about this man. She can't think of a thing to say.

Fortunately, the waiter arrives and Buddy orders a martini for himself, and over her modest demurral, "A glass of chardonnay for the lady."

Then Buddy launches into a tale about his recent hip surgery, and Esther allows that she dislocated her shoulder after tripping on a cord in her living room. "I'm much better," she quickly adds. "But now my daughter has ramped up her campaign to move me into one of those places where you get all your meals. And if you want, they have organized activities. Sing-alongs. Bingo. That sort of thing," she says, dismissively brushing a freshly manicured hand through the air. "I suppose Ceely means well," Esther continues. "She says it's like a cruise. Or maybe I said that." Nervously, she laughs. "Listen to me. Anyway, I'm all right. And," she pauses, scrutinizing Buddy's face, thinking that she detects, beneath the wreckage, the man she would have recognized anywhere. "And you look all right, too," she declares.

The drinks arrive, short-circuiting their confessions of debility. Buddy holds up his glass. "Here's to being all right."

Esther returns the toast and sinks back into the cozy booth, glad to be here with someone who can appreciate a place like the Drake, with all its creature comforts.

Then an awkward silence descends upon them. Esther is wondering whether they've exhausted their conversational bag of tricks when Buddy says, "That's a lovely dress, Esther. Blue becomes you."

She blushes and almost blurts out her plans to be buried in it. But suppose he takes offense or finds it ghoulish that she chose to meet him in her funeral attire? To avoid any misunderstanding, she'd have to explain that it's the best dress she ever owned, that she'd bought it during her svelte phase, and that recently she'd had it altered in accordance with her body's latest revision. But that might lead to a confession of her fantasy double life involving that good-for-nothing Hank Stammler, who left his wife for some hotsy-totsy, long-legged girl who sold cigarettes at the Chez Paree. And that, in turn, might remind Buddy of the time he'd followed her into the kitchen. There are so many landmines lurking here between the heavy cutlery and white table linens.

Their food arrives and after the waiter finishes hovering with his pepper mill, Esther leans across the table and playfully asks, "Whatever happened to pepper shakers?"

Buddy, struggling with his club sandwich, doesn't reply. Esther stifles the urge to reach across and rearrange the sandwich for him, then wonders if she could have managed any better? Seeing Buddy is like holding up a mirror to her own infirmities. She's glad she ordered the mushroom risotto, to which she turns her attention.

"Pepper shakers?" he says, and Esther perks up, ready to fire the next volley across the table.

"Why, I don't know," she says. "I suppose they're just one of those things that have gone by the wayside. Like black-and-white TV."

Buddy looks up at Esther. "Or typewriters," he says. "When was the last time you saw one of those?"

Esther tells him about the old black Royal with pearly keys that she still can't part with. "We used to haul it out of the front hall closet and set it up on the dining room table. My father dictated letters and I typed." She pauses, watching Buddy try to stuff a tomato back into his sandwich, before admitting defeat. After he sets the whole thing down, she continues. "They were complaint letters mostly. He had this need to set the record straight. Once, after biting into a chip of wood in a peanut cluster bar, he wrote to the head of the company and received a box of candy. Then his waterproof watch conked out when he wore it in the tub, but I'm not sure he received a new one. He even wrote to the head of Winnebago, offering to drive one of their vans across the country." She laughs. "As if he'd be doing the company a huge favor. He offered to give free tours to anyone who asked. People would marvel at it. The company's stock would soar." She shakes her head in disbelief. "Marty returned home early one day and saw what we were doing. I didn't hear the end of that for a long time."

"Sonia," Buddy says, as if it were his turn to bring up the name of a deceased spouse. "She, too, has gone by the wayside." He fishes an olive from his drink, slides it off the toothpick with an ease that eluded him with the sandwich. He has nice hands. She can almost remember their touch, and wonders if it's regret she's feeling, regret that she didn't get to know them any better.

"I suppose we could put together quite a list," Buddy says, before popping the olive in his mouth. He proceeds to tell Esther about a developer near Denver with plans to turn a vast stretch of grassland into vacation condominiums. "He wants to build an indoor ski slope. Or an auto-racing theme park." Buddy shakes his head. "You know, there's a certain owl that spends time on that land every year."

"Who ever heard of such a thing?" Esther debates whether to say more, but the thought of so much loss, both real and potential, is too dispiriting. Then, brightening, she says, "But the Drake is still here. And this charming restaurant. Don't you love it?" she says, gesturing with a wave of her hand. "It's like the dowager of Chicago hotels. The Grand Dame. The Queen Mum. When I walked in here, everything felt so familiar." She smiles. "Even the sign on ladies' room door brought me back. Powder Room. You don't see that anymore."

She's become voluble on a few sips of wine. "Listen to me, going on." But Buddy, who is attempting to cut a potato chip with his knife and fork, seems lost again. It's hard to believe this is the man who enjoyed a bad boy reputation. Once, when hosting a dinner party, Esther had gone to check on the roast and as she bent over the oven, she felt a hand on the small of her back. Something in the way that hand inched down to caress her bottom told her it wasn't Marty's. After shutting the door, she turned to confront the owner of the offending hand. Before she knew it, he was kissing her. And she kissed him back.

In the following weeks, she had trouble eating, and once, when she spotted Sonia pushing her grocery cart toward her, Esther turned, went the other way, and hid out near the frozen foods until she was sure Sonia had left the store. Later, on a whim, she stepped inside the Catholic church down the block. With the exception of an older woman kneeling in the second pew, the place was empty. Esther walked around the cool, dimly lit sanctuary, not knowing what she was looking for. Then she spotted something that resembled an ornate phone booth. Her heart pounded as she approached. She had no idea how this worked. Was someone sitting behind the velvet curtain waiting for her confession? What would she say? A dinner guest, the husband of a close friend of mine, grabbed me while I was checking on a standing rib roast. He kissed me and I kissed him back. I kissed him long enough to know that he tasted of gin. I've never done that before, not since I married Marty. And then she burst out laughing, the sound reverberating off the cold stone walls. It was the "summer of love." Young people were running naked at Woodstock. They had sex in the mud, in the open, in front of friends, strangers, cameras. What did they care! Young women burned their bras. They took the pill. Marty's assistant, that lazy mooch, Greenberg, had a wife who was fooling around with her tennis instructor. Still laughing, Esther ran out of the muted church, into the bright daylight. From then on, she steered clear of Buddy Markel.

These thoughts rattle Esther. Her hand flies to her blouse, checking to see that the buttons are secure. She looks down at her plate, pushes the rice around with her fork, hiding out from

Buddy the way she once hid from his wife. What if Buddy has read her mind? But Buddy is still struggling with his knife and fork, attempting to cut a potato chip.

At last, Esther picks up the thread of their conversation. "I didn't mean to suggest that anything—not even this glorious hotel—could compensate for the loss of an owl," she says.

"Of course you didn't." He sets down his knife and fork. "And I agree. This place is grand."

Then they begin listing all the things that had gone by the wayside. "Price stickers on grocery items," Esther says.

"Milkmen."

"Thank goodness for that, or we'd be forced to say milk-persons," Esther jokes.

"Chewing gum for a nickel."

"Peanuts! I bet you didn't get peanuts on the airplane. Food allergies," Esther says and rolls her eyes. "I'll tell you what else has gone by the wayside. People making their fortunes off things. Widgets. You know, stuff we can use." She tells Buddy about a cousin who invented fitted sheets. Another cousin made a fortune selling gloves. "And someone had to invent paper clips. Or paper cups. Recently, I read the obituary of the man who made millions off Toni permanents. How often do you stop to think that someone had to invent the most ordinary things, things that make bigger things run, or like fitted sheets, make life easier? Things that, in a nutshell, do something. Now it's all junk bonds and hedge funds and things we can't even understand, let alone hold in our hands."

Buddy, who has been making another attempt at his sandwich, sets it down and with a confused look says, "Food allergies?"

"Did I say that?" She certainly has gone off on a tangent. "Oh, yes. From the peanuts. They've stopped serving them on airplanes. What I want to know is why the allergic people can't say, 'No, thank you?'"

Buddy nods, though not convincingly, and then not be outdone he says, "Phone booths . . . with doors that shut."

She smiles. "I hadn't thought of that."

"I hadn't either, until I was looking for one. And then I wondered, 'What would Clark Kent do?'"

"I suppose he'd find some other changing room," Esther says. "Or not. In which case." She frowns. "Who would save us from ourselves?"

Certainly not the man seated across from her, who is now reaching for his drink. She holds her breath while he brings the glass to his mouth and then, with surprising aplomb, sets the long-stemmed glass firmly back on the table. Still, Buddy Markel will not be our savior. For that matter, neither will she. We've had our chance, she thinks. Somebody else will have to figure out how to save a world without widgets or spotted owls.

Buddy looks at her intently, and after a long pause he says, "Sonia. Sonia's gone." He reaches for his wallet and after much fumbling slaps a picture on the table as if it were the winning card in a hand of gin rummy. He taps it gently, then strokes the image of a woman with cropped gray hair who is seated on a park bench. "That's Sonia."

"I know," Esther murmurs.

"You do?"

Esther nods, but as she draws the picture closer she wonders if she spoke too soon. The woman in the picture is leaning into a cane. And her stiff, short hair is wrong. The last time they'd met, Sonia had the kind of thick, silver hair that you see on models chosen to make aging look glamorous and fun, like the woman in the Cedar Shores brochure. This woman is wearing a long black skirt, a peasant blouse, and fat amber beads. She is a woman who might be impersonating Sonia. Would Esther recognize her if they were to pass in the supermarket? For that matter, would Sonia know Esther?

"She's beautiful," Esther says, sliding the photo back across the table.

Buddy nods. Then, suddenly, with all the enthusiasm of their initial greeting, he says, "Esther! Esther Lustig! It's so good to see you. How long has it been?"

Oh, what difference does it make? She can tell him, but if they were to sit here long enough, he'd ask her again. She wishes Sonia was here. Sonia wouldn't go all stupid on her.

## Postscript

Two weeks before Esther was scheduled to move into Cedar Shores: A Retirement Community, Ceely received a call from Milo. "Your mother," he said gravely. "She is on bed."

Ceely rushed right over, not knowing whether "she is on bed" meant that Esther had fallen and was on the bed resting, or whether she was on the bed with a fever, or whether she was on the bed unwilling to get up and that Ceely had better come over and talk some sense into her, as she'd done the previous week. Ceely refused to entertain any other possibility.

Soon after Ceely arrived, Sophie showed up with Lenny, who spent most of the time on the couch, his head in his hands. Barry, the last to arrive, was talking on his cell as he strode into the living room.

"She's on the bed," Ceely said to her brother, and then they all traipsed after him into the bedroom, even Lorraine, who had alerted Milo when Esther didn't answer the phone at the appointed time.

Later, Lorraine would tell Ceely, "Now here's the part I can't remember. Whenever we separated, one or the other of us would say, 'I'll call you in the morning.' It was your mother's turn to call, but I don't think she said that."

Lorraine dabbed at her eyes with a crumpled tissue. "We'd been to our class at the community center, the one where we write in journals. Then we went to Wing Yee's, and after, we sat on the courtyard bench," she said, indicating with her head the

183

approximate spot, two flights down, where they'd rested after lunch. "The air was nippy, but the sun felt good."

"Then what happened?" Ceely asked.

"Your mother said, 'I feel sad,' and I said, 'About what?' And she said, 'Everything.' And I said, 'Esther. Be specific. Please.' Then she got a little prickly. You know your mother. 'You want specific?' she said. Then she held up her hand." Lorraine demonstrated how Esther had traced the outline of one crooked index finger with the other. "I was shocked to see how bent her finger was," she told Ceely. "I remember thinking, How could I have overlooked a thing like that? 'The doctor calls it a swan's neck deformity,' your mother said, and I remembered that of course she'd mentioned it, which made me wonder how I could have forgotten. Anyway, she said, 'Swan's neck. Sounds better than it looks. You live long enough, Lorraine, you get the booby prize.' Your mother paused for a while, but she wasn't finished. She said, 'My TV is on the fritz. And I'm having trouble reading the paper. And now Ceely has signed me up for that place. Bingoville.'"

Lorraine's hand flew to her mouth. "I'm sorry." Then she reached for Ceely's hand and patted it. "I don't know what I'm saying."

"Go on." Ceely edged closer to Lorraine. They were sitting on Esther's love seat, which Sophie and her boyfriend would soon be coming to pick up. "I'm just trying to figure out what happened."

Lorraine wiped her eyes again with the shredded tissue.

"Please, Lorraine," Ceely urged. "Tell me what happened next."

"Next? I think that's when she batted her hand in the air and said, 'Enough about me.' And she started talking about a bomb going off in a market in Iraq. 'A father and son had gone to buy a bird. And then. Kaboom! Gone. Just like that.' She told me she'd tried figuring out what she'd been doing when the bomb went off. She'd calculated the time difference. She said it was nine hours ahead in Baghdad. 'So when it's three in the afternoon, I'm just waking up. Or maybe I'm still asleep. Yes. I was probably asleep when that bomb went off,' she said." Lorraine paused. "Then your mother gave me one of her looks and said, 'How's that for specific?' She got teary and looked away, started rubbing her finger, as if she was trying to straighten it out. She said something I couldn't hear. If she isn't looking right at me, I can't hear so good. So I said, 'What did you say?' That's when she looked up, raised her voice so loud I was afraid the neighbors would come running. 'And I'm still here!'"

Lorraine continued. "Then I had to get going. I wanted to bake a cake for my niece's daughter's baby shower. A hazelnut torte. Your mother loved my tortes." She smiled. "Then we parted. But I don't remember hearing her say, 'I'll call you in the morning.'"

Esther never called. So Lorraine called her, and then she called Milo, and then they were all gathered around Esther's bed, shouting, "Mom!" "Nonna!" "Esther!" "Ma!" Even Milo, who had been a paramedic in Belgrade before fleeing to Chicago, who knew that all the shouting in the world wouldn't rouse the tiny figure lying faceup on the white chenille spread, even he joined in. "Mrs. Esther!"

Sophie leaned over to kiss her Nonna's cheek. "She looks so peaceful," she sighed. "Like Sleeping Beauty."

As a child, Sophie had loved taking naps with Esther, snuggling under the comforter, kissing her grandmother's soft cheek, inhaling the lingering sweetness of the Pond's that she lathered on her face every night at bedtime. Esther would lie there, serene, eyes closed, and just as Sophie decided she was sound asleep, her grandmother would pounce and, like an affectionate retriever, lick her face. So when Sophie leaned over Esther's eerily composed body, inhaling a last whiff of the familiar Pond's, she half-expected her Nonna to spring up, plant one of her sloppy kisses and cry, Fooled you!

But the figure in the blue dress was a study in repose. "Still life on chenille," Sophie whispered, eerily echoing a remark Esther had made not that long ago. Then she wondered aloud why Esther was wearing the dress. Softly, she said, "Perhaps Nonna had a premonition."

After all, how many times had Esther cried, "Get out my blue dress and shoes?" And how many times had one or the other of them shot back, "Get it yourself!" All that time, Esther was trying to tell them that she was old; that she wouldn't go on forever. Despite her son-in-law's efforts to extend life, she might have told them that she didn't want to go on forever. But they dismissed her with jokes. "So in the end," Sophie said, "she got the dress for herself." The girl started to weep.

Esther looked as if she might have been heading out for the evening. She'd put on her pearls with the matching earrings, and the Lady Bulova, a birthday gift from Marty. She had on nylon stockings and a fresh coat of lipstick. Her glasses were on the nightstand, and her shoes—the dyed-to-match silk high heels—stood beside the bed, pointy toes facing out.

"She looks perfect," Sophie said, wiping her eyes on her sleeve.

"Too perfect," Ceely replied.

"We don't even know that she's really, you know," Barry mumbled. "Maybe she's just in a deep sleep. I mean, don't you think we should call someone. To confirm?"

"Feel her hand. It's ice," Sophie said, but her uncle recoiled and backed away. "Besides, Milo used to be a paramedic."

Barry looked at the super, as if for the first time. "What's he doing here?"

"Shut up, Barry," Ceely said. Then, "Go ahead. You call. Put that phone of yours to good use."

It was Milo who made the call.

Esther died of natural causes, though for the longest time,

Ceely couldn't shake the feeling that her mother had taken matters into her own hands, that if only she hadn't pushed her mother to move none of this would have happened. Lenny, who hoped one day to find the switch to extend human life, would put his arm around his wife and say, "She wore out, Ceel. That's what happens."

"But the scene was too perfect," she'd say, to Lenny, to Sophie, to anyone willing to listen. "It was so artfully arranged. Like a still life. Sophie was right."

Certainly, Esther had outdone herself in every way. If only her mother could have seen what the others observed. The magazines on the coffee table were fanned out like early morning in a doctor's waiting room. The bathroom sparkled; the towels were freshly stacked. The dishes were put away, except for a single mug, turned upside down in the drying rack. Esther had looped a clean dish towel over the oven handle. With the exception of the spices and odds and ends of rice and grains, she'd consumed all the food in the cabinets and wiped the refrigerator clean. Even the place mats—Esther always set out two, as if Marty might stroll in for dinner at any moment—had been put away.

For years to come, they would all remember Esther's shoes pointing out, as if awaiting their marching orders, and the fact that when her body was lifted and taken away, the chenille spread appeared as taut as a freshly made bed in a five-star hotel. It appeared as if Esther had been levitating, as if she'd willed herself to be lighter than air so as not to disturb the bedding.

I would like to thank the following individuals for their advice, encouragement, and efforts on my behalf: Faith Sullivan, Doug Stewart, Ann Woodbeck, Janet Hanafin, Jean Housh, Sherry Roberts, Don Pastor, Carol Dines, and Daniel Slager.

I owe a special thanks to the Ragdale Foundation for the gift of time and space. Much of this book was written there.

Above all, I am grateful to Bill Price for his insights and comments, but most especially for being there.

*Being Esther* is Miriam Karmel's first novel. Her short stories have appeared in numerous publications. She lives in Minneapolis, Minnesota, and Sandisfield, Massachusetts.

**Reading Group Questions for *Being Esther***

1. At eighty-five, Esther hasn't yet "lost her marbles." What has she lost?

2. Esther believes "she is still herself—albeit a slower, achier, creakier version of the original" (p. 164). And yet, she calls her friend (p. 11) hoping that, "Sonia will remember it all. She'll vouch for Esther's memories; she will validate Esther's existence." Consider how we disappear into old age.

3. Esther's life is presented in a nonlinear way, jumping forward and back in time. How does this affect the reader's understanding of Esther?

4. Esther admires how her friend Helen "could turn her back on tradition" (p. 43). How has Esther defied the constraints of her life?

5. In an apology to her mother (p. 87), Esther realizes that cleaning put her mother "in command," and made her "safe there in a way you never were in the world outside." What has made Esther feel safe? How has she taken command of her own life?

6. Marty, like his watch, was "annoying, yet dependable" (p. 169). How did Esther cope with the emptiness of her long marriage? Why does Esther continue to rely on Marty long after his death?

7. Esther is "content doing nothing" (p. 17) How does this conflict with her daughter's prescription for Esther's well-being? With life in the modern world?

8. In the grocery store, Esther wonders if all the choices there are meant to "balance the losses? To make us forget that every day our lives become a little less full than they were the day before?" (p. 148) How are choices diminished late in Esther's life?

9. "Oy, please," Esther's mother says. "What do you want from me?" (p. 121) Do the mothers and daughters in Being Esther know what they want from one another? What stops them from asking for it? How is Esther's relationship with her mother reflected in the one she has with Ceely?

10. Esther's memories (p. 176) are like "so many landmines lurking here between the heavy cutlery and white table linens." Do Esther's memories comfort or disturb her?

11. Consider the sadness Esther feels when she realizes that her family will not want any of her things when she's gone. What do these possessions represent for Esther? What possessions of yours would arouse a sadness similar to Esther's?

12. Sophie says "My Nonna doesn't think anyone is really happy. 'Who's happy?' It's like her mantra" (p. 162) How has this philosophy protected Esther in her life? How has she challenged her own ideas about happiness?

13. Consider the role "independence" has played in the lives of Esther and her daughter, Ceely. How has Ceely's independence affected Esther differently over the years?

14. Esther tells Marty, "If you talk to someone, they'll talk back. Isn't that what it's all about?" (p. 151) What makes Esther so circumspect in conversation with her family?

15. "That's what people do," Esther tells Fanny Perlman. "They forget where they came from" (p. 171) How is this true for Esther? Her parents? Her children?

16. How did Esther's ideas about death change over the course of the story?

Interior design by Ann Sudmeier
Typeset in Minion Pro
by BookMobile Design & Digital Publisher Services